I'M GOING TO BE FAMOUS

I'M GOING TO BE FAMOUS

Tom Birdseye

A Yearling Book

Published by
Dell Publishing
a division of
Bantam Doubleday Dell Publishing Group, Inc.
666 Fifth Avenue
New York, New York 10103

The trademark Yearling® is registered in the U.S. Patent and Trademark Office.

ISBN: 0-440-40212-3

Reprinted by arrangement with Holiday House, Inc.

Printed in the United States of America

December 1989

10 9 8 7 6 5 4 3 2

OPM

To Nan Phillips, who helped get
the bump off the log

M. K. Wren, who taught the
bump how to write

And most of all to my wife, Debbie,
who believed in bumpy logs
from the very beginning

I'M GOING TO BE FAMOUS

CHAPTER 1

"I've made up my mind."
—ARLO MOORE

The big pine tree in my backyard is easy to climb. From near the top I can see over the houses of Seagrove, Oregon, and down the hill to the Pacific Ocean. There's a forked limb up in the tree that makes a perfect place to sit. From it I can throw pine cones at my pesty nine-year-old sister, Kerry. I can listen to the fog buoy at the end of the jetty, too, or watch for whale spouts, or just sit and think. That's where I am now—up in the big pine, just sitting and thinking.

Today is the last Saturday before school starts in Seagrove. Monday is Labor Day. On Tuesday I begin the fifth grade at Lincoln Elementary School. Me, Arlo Moore, going back to school already. Summer will be over, and just because it's the day after Labor Day. That's a lot to think about.

But that's later. Right now it's still Saturday, and it's still summer. The sun is shining, sister Kerry is nowhere to be seen, the ocean is calm and blue, *and* I've got my copy of the *Guinness Book of World Records* with me. That's a lot to think about, too.

My favorite book of all time is the *Guinness Book of World Records*. There are people listed in it who have done all sorts of incredible things like sleeping on nails, walking three thousand miles on stilts, yodeling for over ten hours, or eating lots of bananas really fast.

I love to eat bananas—anytime, anywhere, any way I can. That's why I've read about the world record for eating bananas so many times that I've got it memorized: a man named Dr. Ronald L. Alkana ate seventeen bananas in only two minutes. He did it at the University of California in Irvine on December 7, 1973. That was before I was born, and it's *still* the world record. I think about that a lot, especially when I'm up in the big pine.

But yesterday I had a new thought. It was one of those thoughts that stuck its nose into my business just like my dog Porkchop does when he's looking for a bone. "Arlo," this thought said to me, "you could eat seventeen bananas in less than two minutes. You should be in the *Guinness Book of World Records* instead of Dr. Ronald L. Alkana."

Well, at first that thought just sat in my brain like my dog Porkchop does on the back porch, not moving a muscle. But today I've been giving that thought some serious consideration. I've turned it over in my mind a couple of times. I've looked at it very carefully. I've spent a lot of time thinking about it, and I've made a decision: I *could* break that record. I *could* be in the *Guinness Book of World Records* and it would be *wonderful*. I'd be on TV. They'd make a movie about my life. I'd be rich. I'd ride in a big, fancy car. My fans would follow me everywhere.

"Hey, Arlo."

I can hear it now, fans calling my name.

"Arlo, it's me, Kerry."

Fame, riches, my name up in lights . . . *wow*.

"Arlo, listen to me."

The world-famous banana-eater, that's me, Arlo Moore.

"Arlo Moore!"

"Huh? What?" I ask, looking down at one of

the last people in the world I want to see.

"Come down out of that tree," sister Kerry orders. "Mom says it's your turn to mow the lawn. You've got to clean up your room, too."

Yep, I've made up my mind. The time has come for me to take action. My path in life is now set. Look out, here comes Arlo Moore, banana-eating champion of the world.

I'm going to be famous.

CHAPTER 2

"Wake me up when you're done."
—KERRY MOORE

"Seventeen bananas? You're crazy, Arlo. You're completely bozo-brained!"

That's the first thing Kerry said when I told her about my decision to break the world banana-eating record. She then told me how I must have been mailed to the wrong house when I was a baby. She said the postman got the packages mixed up and sent her real brother to the zoo in Portland. "He's in a cage there, making faces at first-graders," she added. She grinned at me and said that I must be a chimpanzee disguised as a ten-year-old banana-lover. I'm the only one in the family who doesn't have curly hair, she pointed out.

According to her, my straight dark brown hair and brown eyes prove I'm not her real brother. "You're part monkey, Arlo. I just know it," she said with a laugh.

Kerry thinks I'm crazy for even thinking about trying to break the world record. But she said she'd time me on Dad's stopwatch to see how fast I could eat just one. "It should be a good laugh," she said.

How did I ever get so lucky to have a sister like Kerry?

"OK, Arlo, are you ready?"

"Yeah, I think so, Kerry. Give me just a couple of seconds to get in my best form."

My calculator figures that in order to break Dr. Alkana's record, I have to eat one banana every seven seconds. I can do that. I know I can. I've got banana-eating talent.

I remember last year when Darrin Hays bet me fifty cents I couldn't peel and eat a banana with one hand. *And* I had to do it while swinging on the stall door in the boys' bathroom at school. That was some of the easiest money I've ever earned. I'll bet I could eat a banana in seven seconds while riding my bike backward, or jumping through a flaming hoop, or parachuting....

"Arlo!"

"Huh? What, Kerry?"

"C'mon. Let's get on with this. I want to go watch cartoons."

Kerry doesn't understand the importance of this event. I could be the first person from Seagrove, Oregon to be in the *Guinness Book of World Records*. History could be in the making, and she wants to watch cartoons.

"OK, Kerry, I'm ready. Have you got the stopwatch set on zero?" I ask.

"Yes."

"Do you know how to work it?"

"Yes, Arlo, I'm not dumb," she says, looking . . . well, looking kind of dumb.

"OK, then," I say, "give me the countdown."

"Banana-eaters to your mark!" she shouts. Kerry enjoys shouting.

"There's only one of me, Kerry, and you don't have to shout."

"Listen, Arlo, do you want me to time how fast you can eat your banana or not?" She glares at me.

"Yes, I do."

"OK, then let me do it my way so I can go watch cartoons, or I won't do it at all."

Sometimes I think having curly red hair gives my sister her bad temper. Mom has light brown hair with little streaks of gray she calls "child-rearing hair." Her curls are soft and loose. Dad's hair is blond and wavy, but he combs it straight back to cover his bald spot. My big brother John's hair is just like Dad's, except he has more of it and he parts it in the middle. Mom says I look like my granddad did when he was my age and that's why my hair is straight and darker. But Kerry's is a family mystery. She's got the curliest, frizziest, reddest hair I've ever seen on anybody. My sister, ol' spaghetti head.

"Do it your way, Kerry."

"I knew you'd come around," she assures me. "Banana-eaters to your mark!"

I must concentrate on my banana.

"Get set!" Kerry shouts.

I'll start off easy. I'll eat this first banana in less than ten seconds. Then I'll work down to eating one in seven seconds. *Then* I'll...

"Ready!"

I will cram it into my mouth in one piece and swallow it in one gigantic gulp. This should be a breeze.

"And..."

Look out, *Guinness Book of World Records*, here I come.

"*Go!*" Kerry screams at the top of her lungs.

Hi yo, banana, away!

I have the whole banana in my mouth. It's *big*. It's *too big* to swallow whole. I've made a mistake. I must change my strategy.

"Go, Arlo, go!"

I'm chomping furiously. I'll smash this banana into delicious banana mush in two seconds and suck it into my stomach like a bionic vacuum cleaner.

"Ten seconds, Arlo! Swallow! Swallow!"

Ten seconds. Oh, no, I thought I could do it easily in *less* than ten seconds. My mouth is so full I can hardly chew. Banana mush keeps trying to escape. *Back,* banana mush, *back.*

"Gross, Arlo! You look like a stuffed pig."

I'm chewing as fast as I can. I've got to get this stuff down my throat.

"Twenty-five seconds, Arlo."

Twenty-five seconds. This is no way to get into the *Guinness Book of World Records. Down,* banana mush, *down.*

"Forty-eight seconds and counting," Kerry says with a yawn. "Wake me up when you're done."

CHAPTER 3

"You want to bet on it?"
—ARLO MOORE

The ceiling in my bedroom has a hole in it. The hole got there last May when my model rocket blasted off by accident.

I'm lying on my bed, looking at that hole, and wondering how Dr. Ronald L. Alkana ate seventeen bananas in two minutes.

"Your final time was one minute and thirty-two seconds, Arlo. That's for one banana, only one," Kerry reminds me from her seat on the floor. Can't she see I'm busy? "Maybe you could set a world record at something besides eating bananas," she continues. "Is there a record for eating tennis balls? You could probably do that as slow as you wanted."

Dr. Alkana must have inhaled those bananas whole. If he's a doctor, maybe he knows some fancy medical tricks for eating bananas fast.

"I know, Arlo. Why don't you be the first person in history to eat a motorcycle? We could ride you to school when you got finished."

There's got to be a way. I *know* I can do it.

"Or maybe you could eat a tree and leave. Get it, Arlo? Eat a tree and then *leave*."

What is she talking about? Did she say "eat a tree"?

"I have no idea what you're talking about, Kerry," I say as I roll over and prop myself up on one elbow. "Do you think I should just forget about a world record?"

"Arlo! That's what I've been talking to you about."

She's off the floor and looking at my private things on my desk.

"I think you should set a record eating a tree. Forget about bananas."

"Eat a tree? That's ridiculous! And leave my stuff alone, please."

She doesn't.

"Is it any more ridiculous than you eating seventeen bananas in less than two minutes?" she asks.

"That's not ridiculous." I'm getting a little

angry. I can feel my face getting hot. "I *love* bananas, Kerry. You know that."

She stops and looks at me. "That's true," she admits, "you love bananas. But be realistic. You can't eat *that* many *that* fast. You just can't do it."

"What do you mean, can't?" I ask.

"Just what I said, you *can't* do it."

When someone tells me I can't do something, it makes me want to do it even more. Dad calls that being stubborn. I call it being sure of myself. But what it boils down to is this: I'll be zippered into a hot dog bun before my sister tells me what I can't do.

I sit up on the edge of the bed and look her square in the eyes. "You want to bet on it, Kerry?"

"Bet?" she asks.

"Yeah, you know, like when Uncle Cecil bet Aunt Maude she couldn't stop smoking."

"Oh, yeah, I remember," she says with a grin. "And he caught her smoking in the basement, and she had to clean out the garage and paint the bathroom. Sure, I'll bet."

I've got her now...hee hee. I'll make the bet a good one.

"OK, here's the bet, Kerry. If I can break the record after...let's see...after three weeks of training, then you have to clean up my room and do all the lawn mowing for me. I don't have to do any at all. And if I can't break the record, then I'll do all that work for one year. You don't have to do your share."

"It's a bet, Arlo. Let's shake on it."

It's official. We're shaking on it. There's no backing out for Kerry now. I'll show her I can be famous. I'll prove it to her and anybody else who says I can't. *I'm* going to be in the *Guinness Book of World Records*, and that's a fact.

CHAPTER 4

*"Done, done-done,
or done-done-done?"*
—*"DAD" MOORE*

One Saturday afternoon when Kerry was three years old, she decided she was going to help Dad remodel the kitchen. He was fixing the cabinet drawer by the refrigerator. So Kerry "borrowed" his hammer and "fixed" the kitchen table.

That's why we have an orange plastic tablecloth on the kitchen table now. It covers up the big dents Kerry made with Dad's hammer before he got it away from her.

Saturday night is my night to set the table. I put the plates, glasses, and silverware on that orange tablecloth. It's not such a bad job. I think of it as if I'm playing a game of Monopoly: you've got to get the playing board set up right before you grab everything you can get your hands on.

I can never remember whether the fork goes on the right or the left side of the plate. There's a correct way to do it. Some lady named Emily Post made up the rules for the "Supper Table Game." She figured it makes a difference on how you get your food from your plate to your mouth. She sure never visited our house. Here, you get it from your plate to your mouth very fast if it's something you like and you want seconds. And you get it to your mouth very slow if it's something you don't like. Whether you put the fork on the right or the left of the plate has nothing to do with it.

Still, Mom says we should know the "right" way to set the table and eat. This is so we won't act like idiots when we go out. Personally, I never act like an idiot. She must be thinking about Kerry or John.

We always have hamburgers on Saturday night. It's a family tradition. Dad cooks them. He covers his balding head with a chef's hat that Mom gave him and an apron that says "Come and get it!" in rubber letters across the front. He pretends he's a short-order cook at the Seagrove Cafe. I can imagine him doing that—all six feet, three inches of him standing over the grill, cooking and telling jokes. He says if he ever gets sick of selling car tires, he's going to "slop burgers at the Greasy Spoon." I think if the people who run the Seagrove Cafe knew Dad called their restaurant the "Greasy Spoon," they'd throw *him* on the grill instead of a hamburger.

"Arlo! Step right up here, young man," Dad says. "What'll you have? How about a deluxe burger custom-cooked for you at Pa Moore's Greasy Spoon?"

"Sure, Dad."

"How would you like it," he asks, "done, done-done, or done-done-done?"

Dad always grins and points at the sizzling burgers in the pan when he asks me that question. They're always good no matter how I answer him.

"Just done will be OK, Dad."

"One done hamburger, coming right up!" he says as he flips them over and adjusts the heat.

"Hey, Dad."

"Hey, what, Arlo?"

"Did you ever want to be famous?"

He looks at me for a second. "Sure."

"Really?"

"Yeah. When I was a kid, I wanted to be a

famous explorer. I was going to discover hidden mountain ranges in the jungles of Africa, or uncharted islands, or a huge cave that led to the center of the Earth. Your burger is ready, Arlo. One sizzling sandwich straight from the Greasy Spoon, the best hamburger joint on the Oregon coast."

He sure can cook. Boy, that looks good.

"When did you decide not to be famous?" I ask, trying not to be too pushy.

"I don't know," he says, giving me another look. "I guess that's something I just grew out of. I haven't really thought about it for a long, long time. Come and get it, everybody, dinner is served!"

We are all here now: Mom, Dad, John, Kerry, and me. I sit at the far end of the table. That's because I'm left-handed. If I sit with a right-handed person to my left, we bump elbows. Four years ago, I did that to my aunt Roberta. She had a forkful of spaghetti almost to her mouth. It never made it. She didn't say a thing. She just got up and left. Mom said that the white dress Aunt Roberta had on was brand-new and cost a lot of money. I felt guilty. John thought it was funny. So now I always sit where I can't knock spaghetti or anything else into somebody's lap.

"Arlo, why were you asking me about being famous?" Dad asks. He always wants to know why us kids ask the questions we do.

"No particular reason," I reply. "I was just curious."

"Tell him about our bet," Kerry says with a mouthful of hamburger.

"Quiet, Kerry." I'm giving her my shut-up-or-I'll-get-you look.

"Arlo thinks he's going to be famous, Dad," she continues.

"I said *quiet*, Kerry." My shut-up-or-I'll-get-you look doesn't work on Kerry anymore. Why am I tormented by having such a motor-mouth for a sister?

"What's this bet all about, Arlo?" Dad wants to know.

Thanks a lot, Kerry. I'll help myself to some more potato salad and try to act unconcerned.

"Oh, it's just a little bet Kerry and I made, that's all."

"What kind of bet?" he asks firmly. "You know your mother and I don't approve of gambling."

"It's not a money bet, Dad. It's just... well...uh..."

"Yes, Arlo?" Mom asks.

Mom sometimes seems to know what I'm thinking. She sits there quietly and in her gentle way reads me like a book. That's how well she knows me. I think this is one of those times. I guess I might as well tell the whole story.

"Well, it's just a little bet on how fast I can eat bananas. I'm going to break the world record by eating seventeen bananas in less than two minutes. I've got three weeks to get ready. I think that's September twenty-fourth."

Everyone has stopped eating and is looking at me. Big brother John, the hotshot senior in high school, is grinning like he's in a toothpaste commercial. A little piece of onion is on his chin.

"You're gonna eat *what* real fast, Arlo?" he asks.

John is going to give me a hard time about this, I can tell.

"Bananas, John, bananas."

"And how fast are you going to eat them?"

I didn't like his tone of voice. It makes me mad. I can feel myself getting hot in the face again.

"Fast enough for a world record," I answer, trying to stay calm. "I'm going to eat seventeen bananas in less than two minutes. That will put my name in the *Guinness Book of World Records*. And Kerry will then have to clean my room and do all the lawn mowing for one full year. That's the bet."

John laughs. "Seventeen bananas in less than two minutes? *C'mon*, Arlo."

I knew he'd give me a hard time. No one has any faith in me. I must set John straight.

"That's right. I can do it. I'm going to be famous!"

"You can't do it, Arlo," John says.

There it is again, that word *can't*.

"You want to bet, John?" I ask angrily.

He puts down his hamburger, wipes his chin, and grins. "Sure, why not. I'll bet you all the firewood splitting for this winter—four cords of wood."

"It's a bet. Shake on it," I say as I stand and begin to move around the table to shake John's hand.

"Hold it a minute, kids," Dad interrupts.

He probably wants to bet, too. Well, great. I'll bet *anybody*.

"This is getting out of hand. I want these bets called off."

"Dad! *Why?*" I almost scream in his ear.

"For two reasons, Arlo," he says. "First, your jobs around the house are your chores, not something to win or lose in a bet. Your mother and I expect you to do them as part of your responsibility to the family. Second, I think eating bananas that fast could be dangerous. I don't want you hurting yourself because of stubborn pride over a bet."

I look at Mom. A soft smile crosses her lips. She nods in agreement with Dad.

"But—"

"That's it, Arlo," Dad says. "The bets are off. I don't want to discuss it anymore."

"But—"

"I said, that's *it*, Arlo. The end. No more. Finish your hamburger."

I'm *mad*. I sit back down. I'll show them. I'll break the world record, bets or no bets. I'll be famous. *I'll* be the fastest banana-eater alive.

CHAPTER 5

"I think I'm in love."
—JOHN MOORE

"Psst...hey, Arlo."

"Huh? What do you want, John?"

"Come in here, I want to talk to you."

John is leaning out of the bathroom door.

"You mean come into the bathroom?" I ask. "No, thanks. The last time I did that, you put shaving cream in my ear."

"I won't bother you, Arlo," John promises. "I want to talk to you about our bet."

"You heard Dad," I say. "He said the bet is off."

"Yeah, I know, I know. I'm talking about another bet. Come on in here so we can talk privately."

Should I trust John? That is the big question.

"C'mon, Arlo," he pleads. "I've got to get ready for my date with Michelle. I don't have much time."

Well, I guess I might as well see what he has up his sleeve. Besides, this should be interesting. It's worth the risk. Watching John get ready for a date is like watching Porkchop scratch fleas—there's a lot of action, but nothing seems to get done.

John is shaving. I'm not quite sure why he does this. He only has about twenty hairs on his face, and they're all blond. You can hardly see them. The way he puts that shaving cream on, you'd think he has a beard like Santa Claus.

"OK, John, what about the bet?" I ask, keeping my distance. John is getting too big, too fast. Those long arms can reach out and grab me like a frog does a fly. I *hate* being picked on and always losing our wrestling matches.

"Well...Dad said no betting our chores around the house, right?"

"Right," I answer.

"But he didn't say we couldn't bet something else, right?" John asks.

I can tell this is leading somewhere I probably shouldn't go.

John continues. "So let's just bet something else—OW!"

He's just cut himself again. He'd save himself a lot of blood and pain if he'd just shave without a razor blade. No one would know the difference.

"What do you want to bet, John?" I ask.

"Well...how about an extra-large supreme pizza from Papa Dietro's?"

"An extra-large pizza? Aren't those really expensive? I don't have that much in my piggy bank."

John now has three pieces of toilet paper stuck on his face to soak up the blood from razor nicks.

"I knew you'd back out, Arlo. You can't eat seventeen bananas in less than two minutes. You're all talk and no action."

"You want to bet?" I quickly ask. I'm getting mad again.

"Of course I do, dummy," he says. "That's what I've been talking about. Hand me that towel, will you? I've got to get myself beautiful for tonight. I think I'm in love."

John turned seventeen last week. Mom and Dad must have given him a head the size of a watermelon for his birthday. He thinks he's so handsome that Michelle Angier must believe he hung the moon in the sky. Someday, I'm going to ask her what she sees in him. Besides, that is, his two new pimples.

"OK, John, it's a bet," I say. "An extra-large supreme pizza for you if I lose, and one for me if I win. Let's shake on it."

He grins. "It's a bet, little brother. You've got three weeks to get ready. I'll mark September twenty-fourth on my calendar."

September 24. I can taste that pizza now.

"Hey, you guys, open up! I need some water for my goldfish bowl. Louise and Lionel are swimming around in Dad's coffee cup."

It's Kerry, our wonderful sister.

"Beat it, Kerry," John says. "Arlo and I are having a man-to-man talk."

"Pig feathers, John. You've been talking about the bet."

"How did you know, Kerry?" I ask. "You been spying again?"

Leave it to Kerry to spy on a private conversation. She must be hiding superbionic ears underneath all that frizzy red hair of hers.

She giggles. "Well, I couldn't help but hear. This door is awfully thin. They don't make bathroom doors like they used to, you know."

"They don't make sisters like they used to either, do they, Arlo?" John asks.

For once he's right.

"Aw...c'mon, you guys," she begs, "let me in. Louise and Lionel might die if they don't get fresh water. Besides, I need to talk about our bet, too. I thought you might want to bet a few banana splits, Arlo."

Banana splits. Now she's talking. I *love* banana splits.

"How many, Kerry?" I ask.

"I don't know. How about six?"

Six. I can taste them now. Rich, smooth ice cream, luscious syrup, whipped cream, nuts, mint sprinkles, and a cherry all piled on top of a wonderful ripe banana. *Wow.*

"Is it a bet, Arlo?" she asks, still talking through the door.

How can I resist?

"It's a bet, Kerry," I answer.

I might even eat them all at once. I might even...

"Arlo!" Kerry shouts.

"What?"

"Aren't you going to open the door so we can shake on it?"

I look at John and shrug. "OK, come on in. You can get some water for Louise and Lionel and watch John get ready for his date, too."

John has finished shaving and is now apply-
ing large amounts of Acnehide to his face. I
call it "pimple goop." He fights a never-ending
battle with the evil pimple forces of the deep. I
think they live in his closet and sneak out and
attack when he's asleep.

Next he'll put on enough deodorant to make
my dead tennis shoes smell like perfume. I've
seen this performance before. I think this is
Kerry's first time. She's watching intently.

After the deodorant comes the mouthwash.
John gargles so hard that little droplets come
spraying out of his mouth and splatter on the
mirror. I'll have to brush my teeth while looking at myself through dried gargle spots.

And last, but not least, comes the men's co-
logne. John is sure that smelling like something other than himself is the secret to a
successful date. He then carefully brushes his
hair, trying to make sure every strand is in
place, and—presto—John Moore, ace lady's
man, is ready.

He turns and looks at Kerry and me. A big
smile is on his face. "What do you think? Can
Michelle resist this handsome guy?"

Answering that question truthfully could get
a little brother or sister in trouble fast. I'm still

not sure what someone as smart, friendly, and good-looking as Michelle sees in John.

I think I'll go watch Louise and Lionel swim around in Dad's coffee cup. I'll let Kerry get shaving cream in *her* ear this time.

CHAPTER 6

"We only have one bathroom."
—*"Mom" Moore*

Getting out of bed in the morning is never easy. But today being the first day of school at Lincoln Elementary makes it even harder.

Maybe I should stay in bed. I could cover my head with my pillow and lie here like a big rock. School would start without me. All the kids would sit at their desks. The teacher would say, "Where is Arlo Moore, the kid who loves bananas?" And some kid with thick glasses and purple lips would say, "Oh, Arlo—he turned himself into a rock." And everyone would sigh, and the teacher would say, "Please get out a sharpened pencil and a clean piece of paper."

"Arlo, get up, honey."

It's Mom. She hasn't realized that I'm now nothing more than a rock.

"Come on, dear. Today is a big day, the first day of school."

That's exactly why I am now a silent rock.

"Arlo, get up."

I think she's figured out my plan. She's probably not interested in her son being a rock on the first day of fifth grade.

"Your breakfast is almost ready."

And she probably has figured out how to deal with my plan.

"Or maybe you'd rather eat a blob of cold oatmeal and a piece of burned toast as you run after the school bus you're going to miss."

Yep, I think I'll get up.

Nature calls. I must go to the bathroom. To do this I have to dodge through the dirty clothes, model cars, Monopoly game, and scattered banana peels left around from practicing for my world-record attempt. I do this dodging with the skill that comes from a lifetime of keeping a messy room. I clean it up every week, but it seems to get messy within ten minutes after I'm done. Mom and Dad think it's a problem. They don't realize that only

messy-room-keepers can make the rapid turns,
quick stops, and daring leaps that it takes to get
from the bed to the bathroom before it's too
late. I've had lots of practice. They should be
glad I keep a messy room.

The bathroom door is shut. I've arrived here
from my bedroom obstacle course with little
time to spare. Nature is still calling to me—
loudly. It's Tuesday morning and I'm on the
wrong side of the bathroom door.

"Hey Kerry, you about done?" I ask politely
and in a calm voice.

There's no answer. I can hear the water running in the sink. This lets me know that Kerry
is brushing her hair. Her hair feels like steel
wool. It looks like a porcupine with a perma-
nent, and it makes lots of noise when she
brushes it. She has worn out at least three
brushes this summer trying to straighten that
frizzy red stuff. She does it in the bathroom
with the door shut and the water running so no
one can hear the sound of a brush being murdered.

"Hey, Kerry, hurry up. I need to use the
bathroom."

"In a minute," she says.

In a minute may be too late. I'm no longer
feeling calm. What I'm feeling is pain. Maybe I

should do a favor for all the brushes in the world. Maybe I should mail my sister to the moon.

"A minute is too long. I need in there *now*."

"I'm brushing my hair, Arlo," she says.

"I know you're brushing your hair. I can hear. Hey, listen. I *have* to get in the bathroom. Do you understand?"

"Say please."

Yes. I'll do a favor for all the brushes of the world. I'll do a favor for me also—I'll stuff her into an envelope and send her air mail to the outer reaches of the galaxy.

"Kerry!" I hiss through clenched teeth.

"Say please and I'll let you in, Arlo."

I've lost control. I'm beating on the bathroom door. I've become a wild man filled with the strength of a lion. I'm Bigfoot, about to rip the handle off the door. Then I'll change into *Tyrannosaurus rex,* tearing my sister Kerry into little shreds. I'll be the creature of the black lagoon . . . .

"Arlo, what's going on here?"

Help has arrived. Mom seems calm. I'm most definitely not. In pain I shout, "Kerry won't let me in the bathroom!"

"We all have to share, Arlo. We only have one bathroom," Mom says. As always, calm.

My kingdom for a million bathrooms. Bathrooms in the hall. Bathrooms in the garage, the attic, and the big pine. A million bathrooms everywhere. Nature calls to me. *Very loud* it calls.

"But Mom! I need to be in the bathroom *now.*"

She looks at me. I think she understands.

"Kerry, come on out. Arlo needs to use the bathroom. Hurry up."

The sound of a brush being murdered stops. The water has quit running in the sink. I've been saved, rescued from pain on the wrong side of the bathroom door.

There she is, miserable creature. May the hairbrushes of the world get their revenge. May you go bald at age ten. May you always find the bathroom doors of the world locked. May you...

"Good morning, Arlo."

Miserable creature.

"Good morning, Kerry."

CHAPTER 7

*"I'd swear to it on a
stack of pancakes."*
—BEN HAMILTON

Riding in a school bus makes me feel a little
sick to my stomach sometimes. It's not the motion. It's not that smell that all school buses
seem to have. It's not even the fact that school
buses take you to school every morning. I
guess it's just that I've had some bad experi-
ences on school buses. Or maybe *embarrassing* is a better word.

For example: that bus driver didn't really
have to tell everybody just now about the first
time I rode the bus, the first day of school, the
first time, ever.

"Oh, I remember you," she says. "You're little Arlo Moore. Remember the first time you rode on my bus?"

"Yes. Please don't remind me," I say. She reminds me anyway.

"You were so cute," she says. "On the way home from your first day of school as a first-grader, you sat in the very back seat. You were so small I couldn't even see you back there."

I smile and try to get away down the aisle to a seat. Kids are in line behind me, standing on the bus steps and on the sidewalk outside.

"After I had dropped everybody off and driven the bus all the way to the garage," she says, "I found you."

Everyone is listening. I'm beginning to turn red with embarrassment.

"And there you were, little Arlo Moore, sitting in the back seat. I asked you where you were supposed to get off the bus and you said, 'At the green house.' And I said, 'Which green house?' And you said, 'The big one with my other shoes in it!'"

Kids are giggling.

"And I looked down," she says, "and there you were...."

Some kids are laughing out loud.

"...You had tied your left shoe to your right

shoe with a big knot that you couldn't get undone. You couldn't stand up or walk. You were
stuck back there like a hog-tied grasshopper."

Howls of laughter fill the bus. Trying to
smile, I quickly find a seat. Embarrassing. Very
embarrassing. I should have stayed in bed and
missed the bus. I should have stayed home and
practiced eating bananas.

"Hi, Arlo."

It's my best friend, Ben Hamilton. Mrs. Richardson, my next-door neighbor, thinks Ben and
I look alike. "Why, you two could be brothers!"
she always says. Ben has blond hair. I have
dark brown hair. Ben has blue eyes. I have
brown eyes. Ben is three inches shorter than
me, is right-handed, and talks in a high,
squeaky voice. But Mrs. Richardson still thinks
we look alike.

"Howdy, Ben. How was summer camp?" I
ask.

"Great!" he says, sitting down beside me. "I
just got back last Saturday. We got to go canoe-
ing every day. We had horses to ride, pillow
fights at night, Cokes for lunch, and homemade
ice cream every Sunday night."

"Wow! Sounds nice."

"Yeah, but the best part was that I didn't
even have to see my little sister for four

straight weeks. I felt like I was in heaven."

Four straight weeks without having to see your sister. I've got to talk to Mom and Dad about summer camp.

"Hey, Arlo, what's this I hear about you trying to set a world record eating bananas?" Ben asks.

Motor-mouth Kerry, the bathroom hog, strikes again.

"Who told you that, Ben?" I ask, just to confirm what I already know.

"That's what Kerry is telling everybody. She says you're going to try to eat seventeen bananas in less than two minutes. Then she starts laughing."

I feel embarrassed again. The whole school will know about it before morning recess. People will think I'm nuts, just like Kerry and John do. I'll be the laughing stock of the cafeteria. I'll probably be pelted with open-faced peanut butter and jelly sandwiches and Hostess Twinkies.

"Yeah, well . . . I thought I might give it a try," I say quietly.

"I think it's a *great* idea, Arlo," Ben exclaims.

My ears must be full of orange juice.

"Say what, Ben?"

"I said, I think it's a *great* idea. You can do it. You're the best banana-eater I've ever known. You could eat five bananas in one sitting when you were in the first grade. You can break that record if you try."

"You really think so, Ben?"

"Yep, I sure do," he says with a grin.

He really does think I can do it. My friend Ben believes in me. I can be a hero, not a Hostess Twinkie target. I can be famous, not just another fifth-grade kid. I can be ...

"But you know what you need, Arlo?"

There's always a catch.

"No, what do I need?" I ask.

"You need a trainer," he informs me. "That's what you need. You know, like the pros have. Trainers help athletes get ready to break records."

Ben is pointing to his brand-new three-ring notebook. It's got a clear plastic cover on it with a picture underneath. The picture is of a football player catching a touchdown pass.

"This guy," Ben says, "had a trainer help him get ready to catch touchdown passes like that. That's what you need, Arlo, a trainer ... and I have just the right person in mind."

"Who?" I ask. Maybe he knows somebody I don't know.

"Me!" he says with a big grin on his face.

"You?"

"Yeah, me. I, Ben Hamilton, will train you, Arlo Moore, to break the world banana-eating record. We'll use the Positive Brain Approach."

This sounds fishy to me. "The *what?*"

"The Positive Brain Approach. It's a way to get really good at something. I heard about it from Charlie Swink. He uses it to train for baseball season."

Wow. Charlie Swink is the best Little League baseball player in Seagrove. This Positive Brain Approach must be good.

"How does it work, Ben?"

"It's pretty simple...but it's kinda weird."

Ben is looking at the ceiling of the bus. He always looks up when he's trying to think of the best way to explain something.

"How is it weird?" I ask.

"Well...you have to sorta talk to yourself to make it work."

No problem. I do that all the time.

"What do you say to yourself?" I ask.

Ben is still looking at the ceiling. "Actually, you don't really talk to yourself...you...well, you chant to yourself," he says.

I don't understand. "Chant?"

"Yeah, chant."

"What's a chant?" I want to know. I'm looking at the ceiling, too. I start doing that when I sit next to Ben.

"Charlie Swink says it's something you say to yourself over and over and over again," he answers.

"Are you sure Charlie does this, Ben?"

He answers quickly. "Yeah, I'd swear to it on a stack of pancakes. He told me about it last spring."

Ben has stopped looking at the ceiling. I'm glad. My neck was starting to hurt.

"OK. What do you chant to yourself?" I ask.

"All you do is chant: I can, I can, I can, I can. You say it over and over to yourself. And while you're chanting, you imagine yourself eating bananas just like a record-breaker would."

"Really, Ben? That's *it?* That's all there is to it?"

"Yep. It's the Positive Brain Approach. Charlie Swink calls it the PBA. He says it trains your brain to believe you can do anything you say you can. And if your brain believes it, then you'll probably do it!"

I'm not so sure about this.

Ben looks me right in the eye. "Give it a try, Arlo. What have you got to lose?"

If he he only knew how much I've got to

lose: a supreme pizza, six banana splits, and my pride.

"OK, Ben. I'll try," I say as we pull into the driveway of Lincoln Elementary.

His eyes light up. "Great! We'll meet after school to set up your training schedule. Remember, Arlo: I can, I can, I can, I can..."

"OK, Ben. I've got it. I've got it."

Look out, *Guinness Book of World Records*, the chanting banana-eater is on his way. I can, I can, I can, I can...

CHAPTER 8

"Welcome to the fifth grade."
—MR. DAYTON

Room 11 of Lincoln Elementary School is blue. The walls are made of concrete block. They've probably been painted twenty-three different times in twenty-three different colors. The colors are always very pale: pale green, pale orange, pale yellow, pale purple, pale pale.

Some night I'd like to sneak into this school and paint all of the walls bright colors. I'd splash big buckets of fire-engine red and pumpkin orange and neon green on the concrete block. I'd make the walls into big blobs of bright paint all running together into a rainbow of color.

The teachers and our principal, Mrs. Caldwell, would walk in the next morning and be dazzled by the color. They'd be so dazzled that they would put root beer in the drinking fountain. And they'd serve hot dogs, hamburgers, and pizza for lunch. And they'd let us out for three-hour recesses. And they'd say, "Spelling? Math? Grammar? What on earth are those things?" And we would do strange experiments turning frogs into werewolves and slugs into beans. And after another long recess, the color-dazzled teachers would send us home.

"Pssst...Hey, Arlo."

"Huh?" Oh, it's Ben.

"Over here. Here's an empty seat."

But today, the first day of school at Lincoln Elementary, the walls of room 11 are pale blue.

Ben has found us two seats on the far side of the room where we have a great view of the playground. From here we can sit and watch the crows just like last year. The crows sit on the telephone wires and look down on the playground. If anybody drops a piece of food, they fly down and eat it. I'll take them some bread crust every day at lunch and watch them eat it after recess. I wonder if there is a champion crow. A crow who can eat bread crust on the playground faster than any other crow in the world.

Everyone is being quiet. For some reason, even kids who are loud and into trouble the rest of the year are very quiet and nice on the first day of school. Maybe their parents put some strange medicine in their eggs. They probably bought it at the drugstore. A man with thick glasses and no suntan smiled and handed them a bottle of brown liquid. It had a label on it. It said:

Zip Lip Quiet Syrup—Mix with breakfast on the first day of school.
Dosage—Three drops per child.
Guaranteed to keep kids quiet or your money back.

As I look around the room I see lots of familiar faces. There's Timothy. He's the one who kicked the soccer ball right through the window of the girls' bathroom last year. Mrs. Hammond said he did it on purpose.

And there's Dawn. She always wears socks that don't match.

And there's Eric. He threw his peanut butter and jelly sandwich all the way across the cafeteria in the first grade. It hit the wall with a splat and slid all the way to the floor. Boy, what a throwing arm.

And that man there...that's got to be our

teacher, Mr. Dayton. He's new at Lincoln Elementary. No one knows anything about him. All the Zip-Lip-Quiet-Syrup kids in room 11 are watching Mr. Dayton's back as he writes on the blackboard with yellow chalk:

Welcome to Room 11!
Fifth Grade
Mr. Jim Dayton—Head Cook
and Chief Bottle Washer

"Good morning! As you can see, my name is Mr. Dayton. Welcome to the fifth grade."

Wow, what a mustache. His mustache must stick out two inches on either side of his mouth.

"I would like to start off this morning by calling the roll," he says. "Please answer 'Here' and raise your hand when I call your name. That way, I can begin to learn who you are."

I wonder how long it took to grow that thing. He looks pretty young for a teacher. I'll bet he started it ten years ago, or maybe twenty, or maybe even when he was a baby.

"Brendan Allen."

"Here."

Yep. I have standing before me the man who was the first baby in the world to be born with a mustache. He's probably in the *Guinness Book of World Records.*

"Shannon Douglas."

"Here."

I'll bet his mom and dad were so proud. They probably have a photo album full of pictures of him in his diapers and mustache.

"Guy Duncan."

"Here."

I'll bet he smoked cigars when he was in the first grade. And he always had to pay adult prices to get into the movie.

"Eric Galluci."

"Here."

"Dawn Gunther."

"Here."

"Benjamin Hamilton."

"Here."

And by the time he was twelve, he would get his mustache hairs caught in between his teeth.

"Steven Kenny."

"Here."

And he shampoos it every night and brushes it in the morning.

"Elliot La Bay."

"Here."

"Christa Lovejoy."

"Here."

And when the wind blows really hard, I'll bet his mustache tickles his ears.

"Laura McNeil."

"Here."

"Arlo Moore."

He probably pins it back at night so it won't get sucked up his nose while he sleeps.

"Arlo Moore."

He can probably even comb it down over his lips and talk without anybody knowing it.

"Arlo Moore...is Arlo Moore present today?"

"Pssst...Hey, Arlo."

"Oh, sorry. *Here*."

Wow, what a mustache.

CHAPTER 9

*"That's got to be the dumbest
thing you've ever dreamed of."*
—MURRAY WALLACE

I sign my name like this:

Arlo Moore

I worked a long time on signing it this way.
John says it's not correct cursive. I'm left-
handed. What does he expect? Kerry says I'm
just trying to show off. I wonder what Mr. Dayton will say. He's got a pretty fancy mustache.
It should be OK for me to have a fancy signature.

I'm putting my fancy signature on the first

piece of paper from my new notebook. My name goes in the top right-hand corner. I put the date right under that. And on the top line, in the middle, I'm writing in big letters, "SPELLING."

This is the first spelling test of the year. Mr. Dayton says he wants to give us this test to find out how well we spell.

"I will say the spelling word, use it in a sentence, and then say the word again," Mr. Dayton explains. "You will notice that this test begins with *very* easy words and gets more difficult as we go along. We'll start off with first-grade words, but I'll be giving you ninth-grade words at the end of the test."

OK, I'm ready.

"The first word is *up*. The airplane flew *up* in the air. *Up*."

Got it. No problem. Up, cup, mup, fup, sup. I must shut up and pay attention.

"Number two is *that*. Should we go to *that* store? *That*."

Only if they sell bananas. Bananas by the basketful, bananas by the ton, bananas in a great big pile, man that sounds like fun.... *that*—t-h-a-t. Got it.

"Number three is *it*. I saw *it* fly. *It*."

Boy, this really *is* first-grade stuff. I'll bet I

can practice my Positive Brain Approach while I take this test and *still* do a good job.

"I can, I can, I can, I can..."

I think this PBA is working. I can picture myself eating seventeen bananas in less than two minutes.

"I can, I can, I can, I..."

"Ssh, quiet, Arlo."

"What? Who said that?"

"Quit mumbling to yourself, bozo-head."

I should have known. It's Murray Wallace. He's always more than happy to let you know how stupid he thinks you are. Not that he's smart. He's average: average height, average weight, average brown hair and eyes, and he has an average-size brain. He just thinks he's better than everyone else. Kerry says he should be nominated for the Nerd of the Year Award. I agree. Lucky me, he's in Mr. Dayton's class this year. He's also sitting right behind me. Lucky, lucky me.

"I hear you're going to try to break a world record." Murray leans forward in his seat and whispers. "Eating bananas, isn't it? That's got to be the dumbest thing you've ever dreamed of, Arlo."

"Listen, Murray. I happen to be a great banana-eater," I inform him.

"Sure, and I'm president of the United States."

I don't know why, but I always let people like Murray get to me.

"I'm going to eat seventeen bananas in less than two minutes," I say. "That will put me in the *Guinness Book of World Records.*"

Murray laughs under his breath.

"No, you won't Arlo. You can't eat that fast."

There's that word again: *can't.*

I speak through tight lips. "I *can* break the record."

"No, you *can't.* Don't kid yourself," Murray says as he leans farther forward in his chair.

"Yes, I *can,*" I whisper hotly. I'm mad now.

"No, you *can't,*" Murray hisses.

"YES, I CAN, MURRAY!"

Oops. Everybody is looking at me. Mr. Dayton has stopped the spelling test. *Yikes,* I don't even know what number we're on.

"What's the problem back there?" Mr. Dayton asks. "You're Arlo, aren't you? Arlo Moore?"

"Yes sir." Now I'm embarrassed again, not mad.

"You seem to be more interested in talking, or should I say yelling, than in this spelling test."

Leave it to Murray to get me into trouble. May the fleas of a thousand camels infest your bed, Murray Wallace.

"Oh, it's nothing, Mr. Dayton," I say, trying to sound pleasant. "Murray and I were just having a little discussion, that's all."

Mr. Dayton's mustache is twitching.

"I see. Well, you and Murray can tell me all about it during our morning recess."

Murray and I both protest. "But Mr. Dayton—"

"And number twelve is *strange*," Mr. Dayton says with a wave of his hand and a firm voice. "The man thought it *strange* that his pigs couldn't fly. *Strange*."

Number twelve? Good grief.

CHAPTER 10

"I've already thought about it enough to turn an apple brown."
— ARLO MOORE

Standing here on the playground feels good. Kids are running, playing, and screaming. There's the smell of fresh-mown grass and dust in the air. And I'm about as far away from Murray Wallace as I can get without skipping school.

Murray told Mr. Dayton that I was bothering him during the spelling test. He said that he politely asked me to stop and that I yelled at him. I tried to explain my side of the story, but I was so mad I couldn't say anything the way I was thinking it.

Mr. Dayton looked at both of us. His giant mustache twitched from side to side. Then he told Murray that he could leave. I thought I was in big trouble, for sure.

But Mr. Dayton wanted to hear my side of the story. So I told him about trying to break a world record by eating seventeen bananas in less than two minutes. And I told him about my bets with Kerry and John. And I even told him about the Positive Brain Approach that Ben and I are using. I told him about Murray, and how mad it makes me that everybody is telling me I can't break a world record and that it's stupid that I would even try. I told Mr. Dayton *everything*. Then I stood there like I'd been caught with my hand stuck in the cookie jar. And I waited.

Mr. Dayton looked at me really hard and twitched his mustache again.

"Arlo," he said, "I don't see anything wrong with trying to break a world record."

I think I probably let out a big sigh then.

"But," Mr. Dayton said, "I can't help but wonder why you really want to do it."

That seemed a plain fact to me: I want to do it so I can be in the *Guinness Book of World Records*. I'll be Arlo Moore, world-famous banana-eater extraordinaire. I'll be on TV. I'll be in the movies. I'll win my bets.

"Arlo," Mr. Dayton said.

"Yes sir, Mr. Dayton," I replied.

"Think about why you are doing this. OK?"

That sounded easy enough. I've already thought about it enough to turn an apple brown.

"And don't let this interfere with your schoolwork," he added.

That didn't sound easy. But I figured I could manage to pay better attention in class. And if I never talk to Murray the Nerd again, that would be too soon.

CHAPTER 11

*"That's including the
skins and seeds."*
—BEN HAMILTON

Lincoln Elementary School's cafeteria is big
enough to hold one hundred and eighty students. It's Wednesday, hot-dog day, and I'm
standing in the middle of the cafeteria looking
for an empty seat. There aren't any.

The *Guinness Book of World Records* says
that Linda Kuerth ate twenty-three hot dogs
without rolls in three minutes, ten seconds. All
the kids I see around me are eating and talking
at the same time. I wonder if Linda Kuerth
could talk and eat hot dogs at the same time.

"Over here, Arlo. We can squeeze you in."

It's Ben. You can always count on a friend to
make room for you.

"Thanks, Ben. I was beginning to think I might have to eat standing up," I say as I move over to sit down.

"My mom does that," Ben says matter-of-factly.

"Really?"

"Yeah, she stands by the kitchen counter, reads the paper, and eats a bowl of cereal every morning," Ben says. "She thinks that eating standing up makes it easier for her to go to work. She sits behind a desk all day."

"That's pretty weird, Ben."

"Yeah, I tried it once and dumped a whole bowl of milk and Super Coated Krinkles on my shoes."

Super Coated Krinkles, milk, and soggy socks. I can see Ben now.

"Guess what, Arlo?" he asks.

"What?"

"I went to the library and checked out the latest edition of the *Guinness Book of World Records*. The guy who puts all those records together in the book is named Norris McWhirter. He lives in England. It gives his address and everything. Let's write him a letter."

I'm inspecting my tuna sandwich. Mom always packs me a tuna sandwich.

"Write a letter? What for?" I want to know.

Ben puts down his peanut butter and jelly sandwich and looks at me in disbelief.

"What for? To get information, that's what for. We need to know if there are any special rules to this world-record business. We need to know how we prove that you really broke a record. We need to know whether you can peel the bananas before the two minutes start. We need to know—"

"OK, Ben, OK. I get the message."

"*And* we need to know if the lemons can have sugar on them."

I think I must have missed something somewhere.

"Lemons with sugar on them? What are you talking about?" I ask. "I'm going to eat bananas, not lemons."

"I know that, Arlo. *I'm* going to eat the lemons. Three lemons cut into quarters in less than fifteen point two seconds. That's including the skin and seeds. I'll be in the *Guinness Book of World Records*, too."

I need to get this straight.

"Do you mean you're going to try to break the world record for eating lemons?"

"Yep," Ben says with a grin.

"Including the skin and seeds?" I ask.

"Yep," he says with an even bigger grin.

"That makes my teeth curl just thinking about it," I say.

"You eat bananas. I eat lemons."

Ben's voice gets squeakier when he's excited.

"We'll set world records on the same day— September twenty-fourth. How about it?"

It might be nice to have some company on my lone quest for fame and glory. At least Ben believes in me.

"OK, Ben. Let's go for it. You and me, buddy, Seagrove, Oregon's first entries into the famous *Guinness Book of World Records*. *We're* going to be famous!"

CHAPTER 12

"Let me know if I can help."
—LAURA MCNEIL

It's funny, but last year I considered girls to be one of the things in life you just have to put up with, like rain on your birthday, a younger sister, or cough syrup.

But this year it's different. It's like I caught some strange, exotic disease over the summer. All of a sudden, girls are very interesting to me. I think that maybe I've spent too much time with big brother John. Next thing you know, I'll be pretending I shave and start using scented underarm deodorant.

But whatever the reason, I can't help the way I feel. Every time I get around Laura McNeil, my face turns hot like I'm hanging upside down. And I start bumping into things and forget how to talk.

Laura McNeil...I get goose bumps just thinking about her. She's new in town. She's in Mr. Dayton's class. She sits right in front of me. And she's *beautiful*.

"OK, Arlo, we're almost ready," Ben says.

Ben has a very serious look on his face. He's thinking about training for a world record, not about girls. When I look at Laura McNeil, I see gorgeous blond hair, beautiful blue eyes, and a smile that makes me feel sort of dizzy. When Ben looks at Laura McNeil, all he sees is someone who has a brand-new digital wristwatch, complete with calendar, alarm, and a stopwatch button.

That's why I'm sitting across table number 4 in the Lincoln Elementary cafeteria from Laura McNeil right now. Ben asked her to time us on her new watch as we train for our world-record attempt. I'm supposed to sit here in front of the prettiest girl I've ever seen and stuff bananas in my mouth. I'm so nervous, I probably can't even talk, much less eat fast.

Laura looks right at me with those blue eyes.

"Hi, Arlo," she says. "Tell me about this world-record attempt you and Ben are training for."

My mouth is dry. My tongue feels like a sponge. I hope I don't say anything stupid.

"Yeth...uh...wrrr...wrrr..."

I've got to pull myself together. Maybe I should talk fast.

"We're going to try to set new world records," I blurt out. "I'm going to eat seventeen bananas in less than two minutes. Ben will eat three whole lemons in less than fifteen point two seconds, including the skins and seeds."

That was probably world-record talking speed. I wonder if Laura had her stopwatch going. At least I answered her question, though.

"That sounds exciting," she says with a smile.

I think I just melted, dripped out of my seat, and am now a big puddle of Arlo Moore on the cafeteria floor.

"You think so? Really, Laura?"

"Yes, I do. I'm interested in setting a world record, too—in politics."

"Politics?" I ask.

"Yes, I want to be the first woman president of the United States."

She wants to be president of the United States? I watch the news. I know what kind of job being president of the United States is. It's the kind of job that turns healthy men into raisin cakes and smart people into flat tires. You've got to have lots of courage to do that job.

Hmm...our first woman president—Laura McNeil. I get more little goose bumps just thinking about it.

"C K, Arlo, we really *are* ready now," Ben interrupts. He's fidgeting around with his lemons. He keeps standing up and then sitting down every couple of seconds. He's nervous. This is our first training session in front of a crowd. Table 4 is surrounded by kids waiting to see us perform. It's Friday, September 9, and we only have fifteen days before the big event.

I'm nervous, too—about Laura McNeil being here, and about performing in front of a crowd. I guess I haven't been practicing my Positive Brain Approach long enough to be cool, calm, and collected in a situation like this. If I'm going to be famous, I'd better learn how. Maybe a little PBA would help right now:

"I can, I can, I can, I can..."

"OK, you guys. I've got my watch set on zero," Laura says.

My PBA seemed to help a little. But I need more. I need extra help. I need superpowers.

If I were an alien from outer space, that would help. I could be Xexus, superalien, bionic banana-eater from the planet Zoidtron. I'd be from the outer reaches of the Milky Way galaxy. I would come to Earth disguised as a mild-mannered fifth-grader. No one would suspect that beneath this ordinary-looking exterior lurks the fantastic food-gulping talent of Xexus. Champion of the light-speed restaurants of the universe, hero of the macaroni-and-cheese intergalactic wars, leader of the Banana Revolution in deep space, I would stand (er, sit) ready to wow these inferior Earth children.

"I'll say, 'Take your mark, get set, and then go,'" lovely Laura says.

But my problem is that I don't feel like Xexus from Zoidtron.

"Take your mark."

And I don't look like Xexus from Zoidtron.

"Get set."

But I've got to *be* Xexus from Zoidtron.

"And..."

For my planet and the universe, I, Xexus from Zoidtron, will excel.

"Go!" Laura commands us.

Five, four, three, two, one ... *blast off*.

"Yahoo! Go, Arlo! Go, Ben!" the crowd yells.

Down, luscious banana, down. I'm biting

and gulping like a moose who loves chocolate.

"Five seconds," Laura reports.

"Eat, eat, eat!"

The crowd is going wild. I'm almost done. The last bite is going...going.

"Nine seconds," Laura says.

...and gone. The last bite hits belly bottom with a thud. Xexus from Zoidtron is full.

"Nice going, Arlo. Great job, Ben," kids are saying as they pat us on the back. Laura looks at me with that smile that makes me dizzy.

"You finished in twelve point nine seconds," she says. "Ben was right behind you. You know, you two just might get into the *Guinness Book of World Records*. Good job, you guys."

"Thanks, Laura," I say as once again I get goose bumps, feel hot in the face, and begin to melt.

"Sure, Arlo," she says. "Let me know if I can help some other time."

Burp...I think that I, Xexus from Zoidtron, am in love.

CHAPTER 13

"We're a team now."
—KERRY MOORE

It's against the rules to run down the pale green halls of Lincoln Elementary School. My friend Ben, however, has been able to get around this rule. He can run without really running.

When the bell rings at the end of the school day, Ben is usually the first one out of room 11. He shoots out into the hall like a cat out of a washing machine, and the action begins.

Mrs. Caldwell, our principal, plants herself in the center of the hall, outside her office door. She's short and wide, which makes her look a lot like a Japanese sumo wrestler with a dress on. Just her standing in the middle of the

hall with a scowl on her face makes most kids
slow down their headlong rush to be first in
the bus line. But not Ben.

Ben moves down the hall like a sneaky road-
runner, his legs moving in quick little steps.
His head and eyes don't bounce. His feet don't
slap the linoleum floor. He just weaves his way
through the crowd, expertly zipping in and out,
and sneaks by Mrs. Caldwell with a smile on
his face before she can figure out who it is
that's moving so fast. *And* he can even talk
while doing it.

"Hurry, Arlo," he says as he rockets past me
and slips in behind Mrs. Caldwell. "If we get
in the bus line first, we can sit in the back
seat."

"Save me a place, Ben. I'm moving slow
today. I want to conserve my strength for banana practice this afternoon."

"OK, see you on the bus," he yells over his
shoulder.

Besides, I still feel like I swallowed a can-
nonball. One banana speed-eating practice was
enough at lunch. I shouldn't have let the
crowd talk me into doing it three more times.

But a famous person must sacrifice himself
and go beyond the ordinary to prove his worth.
Murray Wallace kept saying that I couldn't do

it again that fast and that I'd never eat seventeen bananas in less than two minutes. I *had* to keep going. I ate the fourth banana in 10.4 seconds.

Speaking of Murray the Nerd, there he is. Wouldn't you know I'd have to stand behind him in bus line.

"Hi, Murray. Say something polite... please," I say, trying to fake a smile.

"Oh, Arlo, it's you. I wanted to tell you how stupid your banana-eating show was at lunch today."

It never fails. Murray will always be a nerd.

"Thanks, Murray. You're too kind," I say and turn away.

"I'm curious, Arlo," he says. "How does it feel to make yourself look like a slobbering pig in front of everybody?"

There are 200 million people in the United States of America. *Why* do I have to live in the same town as Murray the Nerd? The question that now confronts me is whether or not to argue with him. It's usually a waste of time, and I end up getting mad. I'm not sure I have the energy.

"You seemed to enjoy it, Arlo," he continues. "You actually seemed to enjoy making a com-

plete fool out of yourself in front of everybody."

Maybe I'll get some energy. Maybe I'll turn
into Xexus from the planet Zoidtron and blast
Murray into hyperspace.

"I know Laura McNeil thought it was disgusting. Don't you think she did, Arlo?"

"What do you mean by that, Murray?" I ask,
turning to face him.

"I saw her," he replies. "She was watching
you cram bananas in your mouth like a starving
monkey. And timing you! I'm sure she thought
it was disgusting and dumb."

Laura McNeil doesn't find me disgusting *or*
dumb. She wanted to be my partner in science
class this afternoon. She thinks it's exciting that
I'm trying to break the world record.

"I guess it doesn't really matter, Arlo," Murray says with a grin that makes my stomach
twist. "I think she's interested in more of a
man, anyway."

"*What?*"

"You know, Arlo, more of a man—like
me..."

I think I may get violent...either that or
sick.

"...rather than someone who gets attention

by cramming bananas in his mouth as fast as he can."

I am losing my temper. I can feel my face getting hot. My fists are clenching.

"I wonder if Laura would like to meet me at the movies on Saturday afternoon. What do you think, Arlo?"

I'm a volcano about to erupt. I'm a tornado coming down from the clouds. I'm a tidal wave crashing toward the beach. I'm about to *AT-TACK*.

"Hi, Arlo. Say, you look red in the face. You feeling OK?"

It's my frizzy-headed sister.

"Don't bother me, Kerry. I'm about to commit unpardonable crimes upon Murray's head."

Kerry looks at me and then over at Murray. My enemy has somehow slipped into the back of the bus line. He's out of my reach, but not for long.

"Out of the way, Kerry," I order her with my best military voice. "Murray is under attack."

"That sounds like a great idea. But first let me tell you the good news," she says, stepping completely in front of me, barring the way.

"The good news? What good news?" I ask, without taking my eyes off my prey.

"The good news about breaking world records. I'm going to try, too!" She grins at me.

"*What?*" I glare at her.

"And so is Mike."

"*Mike?*"

"Yeah, you know, Mike Snead," Kerry says. "He's just a fourth-grader, but he can eat like an elephant."

She's looking up at me with her idiotic smile going full blast and her red hair shooting out in a thousand different directions.

"Kerry, please don't bother me right now," I plead. "You're breaking my concentration."

Where was I? Oh, yeah, ATTACK.

"What do you think. Arlo? Aren't you glad to have some company on your lonely quest for a world record?"

I can't believe this. Who invented little sisters anyway?

"Kerry," I say with a sigh. "It's not a lonely quest for a world record anymore. Ben is doing it, too."

"But wouldn't it be exciting to have some *more* company on your lonely quest?" she asks. "You know, sort of a team effort. You eating bananas, Ben eating lemons, Mike eating ice cream, and me chewing gum!"

"Kerry!" I almost shout.

"Yes, Arlo," she replies with her big grin shining from ear to freckled ear.

"Can't you see I'm busy?"

"You're not busy," she explains. "You're talking to me. I have your complete, undivided attention. You're excited about having Mike and me in on the Lincoln Elementary World Record team, remember? You're Arlo Moore, my wonderful brother, and you're *not* going to commit unpardonable crimes upon Murray Wallace's head, even though he deserves it. *Because* here comes our beloved principal, Mrs. Caldwell, who will chop you into little pieces and send you air mail to Mom and Dad if you do."

Good grief. How can I zap Murray the Nerd into hyperspace with all of these distractions?

"You do see Mrs. Caldwell, don't you, Arlo?" she asks.

"Yes," I answer, "I see her."

"Good," Kerry says with an even bigger grin. "The buses are here. It's time to go. Just ignore Murray. He's not worth the effort. Save your energy for banana-eating. By the way, you don't mind if Mike and I come over to Ben's for practice this afternoon, do you? Of course, you don't."

This is all I need: a spaghetti-headed sister

who can't stop her motor-mouth.

"We're a team now, Arlo, one big, happy, world-record-breaking family! Isn't this *exciting?*"

"Yeah...sure, Kerry. I'm tingling all over."

CHAPTER 14

"Melon seeds?"
—MICHELLE ANGIER

Ben and I put on regular training performances in the cafeteria. We've been doing it for a week now. Despite what Murray said, Laura McNeil times us on her digital watch. But I saw her talking to him at the playground yesterday. And Ben said that Andy Phillips said that Dawn Gunther said that Murray said that he sat beside her at the movies last Saturday. I don't know, but it all makes me churn inside.

So far this week, I've eaten thirty-seven bananas! That makes me churn inside, too. Kerry says I'm starting to turn yellow around my fingernails. John says I smell like a chimpanzee.

Ben has eaten so many lemons he walks

around with his lips in a continuous pucker. He looks like one of those kissing fish in an aquarium. We're both improving our times, though.

Kerry and Mike Snead come to practice at Ben's garage every afternoon. Mike can really put away the ice cream. He ate a whole quart of mocha almond fudge in less than four minutes on Thursday. He's good. I've got to admit that. I guess I could eat pretty fast, too, if I had a belly as big as a snake that swallowed an elephant.

But then we looked up the record for ice-cream-eating in Ben's *Guinness Book of World Records* again. There's a picture of this guy. His name is Tony Dowdeswell. He ate three pounds, six ounces of unmelted ice cream in 50.04 seconds. That's three quarts.

I don't think Mike can do that. I told him what I thought. He told me that if Tony Dowdeswell could do it, so could he. Then he went home. He said he had a headache.

But as it turned out, Kerry ended up with the worst headache of all. We all figured she knew what she was talking about when she said that there is a world record for chewing gum. I should have known better. We discovered she hadn't even *looked* at the *Guinness Book of*

World Records. We found out it has a paragraph in it about "potentially dangerous" things that aren't accepted for the record book anymore. It listed eating live ants, goldfish, marshmallows, raw eggs in the shell, or chewing gum, and riding bicycles.

I felt sorry for Kerry. She'd been at Ben's every day, chewing away like a cow at a scary movie. She was chewing so hard, her jaw got sore. She used the same gum. ABC gum—Already Been Chewed; over and over and over.

I must admit that her method for saving ABC gum was pretty creative. She would stick it on the inside of the lamp shade when she went to bed at night. Then, in the morning, she'd turn on the lamp and let the heat from the light bulb get her ABC gum warm and soft for chewing.

She almost started crying when she read the paragraph about "potentially dangerous" things. Then she went home and locked herself in the bathroom. Mom thought she might be getting sick, or maybe something terrible had happened at school to make her so depressed. That's one of the reasons Mom dropped us off at Papa Dietro's Pizza Parlor to pick up a pizza for tonight, and then went to get some ice cream for dessert. Mom can't read

Kerry's mind as well as mine, but she knows that nothing cheers her up faster than one of Papa Dietro's super-supreme deluxe pizzas without anchovies, and vanilla ice cream for dessert.

Standing here at the counter, waiting to pay the cashier, I noticed the price went up another $1.25. I'm glad Mom gave me the money to pay for this. Training for a world record is expensive. It takes all of my weekly allowance. I can't afford pizza, now or later.

"Pssst, hey, Arlo," Kerry whispers.

"Huh? What, Kerry?"

"Look over in the corner," she says, obviously feeling better already.

Speaking of pizza, who should appear? None other than my big brother, John. And he's got Michelle with him. She sure is pretty. Dad says she has "sparkle." I think that means he likes her. Maybe he thinks she can do something about John. *Somebody* needs to do something about John, that's for sure.

"Arlo, let's go over and say hello," Kerry whispers. She can't resist spying on John.

"Let him alone, Kerry. He doesn't want you snooping around."

"But Arlo, he might need some help," she says, sipping a Coke.

When Kerry says "help," what she really means is a hard time.

"He doesn't need your help, Kerry. Believe me. He can botch things on his own."

"But we should at least go over and say hello. He *is* our brother, you know. C'mon, Arlo."

Why am I so easily led astray?

"OK, Kerry, but just to say hello. And don't ask any dumb questions or talk too much."

"Dumb questions? Talk too much? Me?"

"So, Arlo, how's the banana-eating going?" John asks.

"Arlo is doing great," Kerry answers for me. "You should see him eat those bananas. Pow, pow, pow. They just fly into his mouth."

"It's going OK," I add quietly, wishing Kerry would shut up.

John and Michelle look at each other and smile. I think I see the "sparkle" Dad talks about. It's in her eyes. But why waste sparkle on John? That is one of the great mysteries in my life.

"You only have a couple of weeks before your world-record attempt, don't you?" Michelle asks. "Are you going to be ready, Arlo?"

"He'll be ready," Kerry blurts out. "I'll be ready, too."

What's this? Has she already forgotten about the gum?

"Ready for what?" John asks.

Kerry replies matter-of-factly. "I'm going to spit melon seeds for a world record."

"Melon seeds?" John asks.

"Melon seeds?" Michelle asks.

"Melon seeds?" I ask.

Kerry is grinning from ear to ear. "Yep, melon seeds. They don't have gum-chewing records in the *Guinness Book of World Records*, but they do have melon-seed-spitting records: sixty-five feet, four inches!"

That's twice the length of room 11 at Lincoln Elementary School. I'll bet that's as long as 150 hot dogs laid out end to end.

"Kerry, do you know how far that is?" I ask.

"Sure, I know," she says, looking at me as if that's the stupidest question I could have possibly thought of. "No problem. I can do it. You've always said I had a powerful mouth, right?"

John and Michelle are both giggling.

"Well, yeah," I admit, "but—"

"So what better way to use a powerful mouth

than for spitting melon seeds for a new world record?" Kerry says with a smile.

"But Kerry—"

"I'll be famous!"

"But Kerry—"

"I'll be in the *Guinness Book of World Records!*"

"But Kerry—"

"I'll be a hero, an idol, a tribute to my school, my city, my state, my country, the *world!* Just like you, Arlo."

Kerry has lost contact with reality. I am an experienced banana-eater. She hasn't trained. She hasn't put in the years of practice. She doesn't understand the dedication, sacrifice, and pain it takes to be a hero. I, Xexus of Zoidtron, have special powers. I understand these things. I can be famous. I can break the world record. I will use PBA and my superalien powers. I will show everyone who's king. This honor belongs to *me*—and *me* alone, not Kerry.

"You can't do it," I tell her.

She turns and faces me. There is not even a hint of a smile on her face.

"Why?" she asks with her hands on her hips.

"You don't have the powers. You just can't."

"Can't?"

"Right, you can't do it," I repeat.

"Can't?"

Kerry must be having trouble with her bionic ears.

"Yes, I can, Arlo, you turkey!"

She's not, however, having trouble with her bionic mouth.

"Quiet, Kerry," I say, looking around to see if people are watching.

"Don't tell me to be quiet! Don't tell me I can't!" She glares at me.

Everyone is looking over at us. John keeps saying, "ssh, ssh." Michelle looks embarrassed.

"I can do it, Arlo! Do you hear me?"

Kerry has gone off the deep end of the bathtub. She hasn't done this since she was in kindergarten and Mrs. De Witt told her she couldn't color the giraffe purple. It had to be yellow and brown.

"Yes, Kerry," I say, "everyone in Papa Dietro's can hear you."

"I can do it!"

She's banging on John and Michelle's table.

"I'm going to be famous!"

Their Cokes and pizza are jumping around on the bouncing table like they're made of rubber.

"I . . . !"

Bang, bang. There's no stopping her now.

"CAN . . . !"

Bang, bang. She just has to get this out of her system.

"DO IT!"

Bang, bang—*splash*. John and Michelle now have a twelve-inch supreme pizza topped with eight ounces of Coca-Cola and all of the ice from Michelle's cup.

And John is *mad*. "Now see what you've done, Arlo!"

"*Me?*" I ask. "What do you mean, John?"

"You got her all worked up," he fumes.

"She got *herself* worked up," I fume back.

"But you started it. You and all this world-record baloney. You're both crazy," he says, pointing at us. Michelle is wiping off the pizza with napkins. "Neither one of you can break a world record."

"But John—" I say.

"And you're going to buy me *two* supreme pizzas when you lose the bet. The second one to replace this soggy thing," he says, standing up. "C'mon, Michelle. Let's get out of here. You've probably seen enough of my *strange* family."

I beg to be heard. "But John—"

I wonder if there's a world record for eating your own words.

CHAPTER 15

"Crows are patient."
—ARLO MOORE

Today is Monday, September 12. Room 11 is getting ready for SSR. Mr. Dayton says *SSR* stands for Sustained Silent Reading. *Sustained* means we don't stop reading for twenty minutes. *Silent* means there is no talking—as in *absolutely* no talking. And *Reading* means that that's what we do—read. We do SSR right after recess. Mr. Dayton says it helps to calm us down and get us used to being back in the classroom.

I think we should change it to SSE—Sustained Silent Eating—as in quietly eating bananas. I have twelve more days left to train for the big event.

Speaking of bananas, where is my banana? Oh, no. I left it out on the playground. It's in my backpack with my *Guinness Book of World Records* and my leftover tuna sandwich. I must go to the rescue.

"Mr. Dayton?"

"Yes, Arlo."

"May I go out and get my backpack?" I ask. "I left it behind the soccer goal. It has my SSR book in it."

"OK, Arlo, but be quick about it," he says, loosening his tie. "We start SSR in two minutes."

"I will. Thanks, Mr. Dayton."

Under my *Guinness Book of World Records*, I find the remains of my tuna fish sandwich. Partly eaten, it lies near death in the bottom of my backpack. I think I hear it calling to me. In its last dying breath, it begs to be fed to the crows. Anything but the garbage can. I'll grant my faithful sandwich its last wish. With great ceremony, I lift it from my backpack and place it on the ground.

"Pssst... Hey, Arlo." It's Ben.

"Huh?"

"The crows, look at the crows."

From the window of room 11, I can see the

crows. They have seen my tuna sandwich. They swoop down from the telephone wires, one by one, gliding onto the soccer field. They walk around the sandwich, eyeing it. I think they're not sure if it's alive or dead. Crows are patient. They'll make sure before they eat.

But I'm not feeling so patient. I can't wait any longer for my banana. This is SSR, not SSE, so I'll have to be sneaky. I'll have to read and eat at the same time.

Slowly, I reach into my desk and gently undo the clasp on my backpack. Very carefully, I raise the flap just enough to slip my hand in. I check the room to see if anyone is watching. Mr. Dayton's mustache is twitching as he reads. My fellow fifth-graders are reading silently for twenty sustained minutes. Now is the time for action.

Gently I probe. With the hands of a pro, I seek out the golden, delicious fruit. *Bingo*, I've struck pay dirt. Once again, I check the room for safety. Looking carefully at my *Guinness Book of World Records*, I slowly pull my practice banana from my desk. Success. I will dine on banana and watch the crows.

The crows have decided it's time to eat. I agree. They're hopping around, pulling bits and pieces of the deceased sandwich apart. I'm performing the ultimate banana feat. I'm peeling my banana with my right hand—and I'm left-handed.

The crows jump in at the sandwich, fight for a piece, and fly a few feet away to eat. They're always trying to outdo each other, sneak a piece when no one is looking, or steal a bit from another crow. What a weird way to eat.

Luckily, no one is jumping at my banana. I don't have to fight for a piece. All I have to do is peel my banana with one hand. No problem for an expert. Ah... finished.

Carefully, I break off a piece. Raising my *Guinness Book of World Records* from my desk toward my face, I smoothly pop my piece of wonderful banana goodness into my mouth and chew, chew, chew, swallow. Not bad. I'm getting faster all the time.

"Excuse me, Arlo, but are you eating?"

Aiyee! It's Mr. Dayton.

"Uh... well... I... yes... yes sir, Mr. Dayton, I am," I stammer, caught in the act.

"Bananas have a strong odor, Arlo," he says, standing beside my desk, looking down at me. "I could smell it all the way up at my desk."

I shift in my chair and wish I could just run away. I feel like a bug trapped in a jar. "You could? Really?" I ask.

"Yes. It's not hard for a banana-lover to smell his favorite fruit."

Do I detect a smile under that mustache? "Are you a banana-lover, Mr. Dayton?"

"Yes," he replies, "but I don't eat them during SSR. It's Sustained Silent Reading, not Sustained Silent Eating."

Good grief, I think he can read my mind, just like Mom.

"This won't happen again, will it, Arlo?" he continues, his mustache twitching.

"No sir," I assure him.

Whew, saved by the understanding of one banana-lover for another.

"Oh, Arlo," Mr. Dayton says.

He's probably changed his mind. I'm about to be sent to Mrs. Caldwell's office.

"Yes, Mr. Dayton?"

"This world-record business, it's just for fun, right?" he asks with raised eyebrows.

"Well, yes sir, but—"

"Good, good. I just wanted to be sure. As long as you've got the right attitude, I wish you all the luck in the world," he says as he turns to go back to his desk.

"Thanks, Mr. Dayton." I sigh with relief.

I can, I can, I can, I can...

* * *

CHAPTER 16

"What are friends for?"
—MURRAY WALLACE

Sophie Zacker thinks I've gone insane. She was the only person in the hall when I quietly snuck out of room 11. She's the only person who saw me slink into the boys' bathroom with two bananas sticking out of my pockets. She stopped and watched me go. Then she went on to her classroom.

Lucky for me, she's the quietest kid in all of Lincoln Elementary School. She won't tell anybody about my secret banana practice place. She never tells anybody about anything.

So now I'm hiding in stall number 1 of the boys' bathroom. Stall number 1 is right by the wall. I picked it on purpose. It has several ad-

vantages over stalls number 2, 3, or 4. First, it's
in the corner of the bathroom. Some kids even
forget that stall number 1 is here because it's in
the corner and behind the bathroom door
when it opens. That's good.

Another advantage of stall number 1 is that it
has a wall on one side. If someone is going to
peek underneath at you (which happens a lot),
he can only do it from one side. This cuts the
chances in half of someone looking under stall
number 1 and catching me practicing my
banana-eating. I like those odds.

And probably the best advantage of stall
number 1 is that the latch on the door works
really well. The other stalls have latches that
are all the time coming undone. You can be
sitting there, minding your own business, and
all of a sudden—*click*, the latch comes undone
and the door swings open. Now *that* can be
very embarrassing.

I have nine days left until I make my attempt
at a world record. Nine days, that's all. I've
been practicing at Ben's, in the cafeteria, and
also secretly at home and in the boys'
bathroom. And I've been doing PBA over, and
over, and over. It's getting so I go to sleep
doing PBA. And then I wake up doing PBA. I
even dream PBA.

Last night I had a weird dream. I dreamed that I walked into a banana factory. There were shiny metal machines everywhere. PBA was blaring out over loudspeakers. A man in a white coat, white pants, white shoes, and a white hat walked up to me. He explained that this was Crystal Murkele's Banana Corporation. He said that bananas no longer grew on trees and that those machines could produce over 250,000 bananas per day. My job was to be a banana taste-tester. I would put my banana taste buds to work on machine-made bananas twelve hours a day, seven days a week. I could retire from the job when I was eighty-three years old.

He smiled when he finished talking. He had yellow teeth. Then he raised his hand over his head and clicked his fingers three times. With that, all the machines in the factory started wheezing and grinding and churning. Bananas began to pop out everywhere: from chutes, pipes, conveyor belts, glass tubes, and chrome tunnels. Before I could even move, bananas were piling up around my ankles. Within thirty seconds they were knee deep. And less than two minutes later, I had bananas up to my eyeballs.

The man in the white coat smiled at me with

his yellow teeth. "Get to work, Arlo," he said, "and be sure to pick up the peels when you're finished."

That dream was so real I woke up with banana taste in my mouth. I even had a couple of banana peels lying on my pillow. I must have fallen asleep right after I did my last timed banana practice.

But now I'm hiding here in stall number 1 of the boys' bathroom. I want to get in one more banana practice before the school day ends... and I want to do it alone.

So here goes. First, a little Positive Brain Approach, brought to me by shortwave brain train, channel 9.

I can, I can, I can, I can...

Second, I must change identities. And so I, Arlo Moore, fifth-grade boys' bathroom outlaw, become Xexus, super banana-eating alien from the planet Zoidtron.

Mission control to Project Bananazap: stand by for blast off. Five, four, three, two, one... Hi yo, banana, away!

I'm taking small bites. With the skill of many hours of practice, I'm hurtling bite-sized banana bits into the outer reaches of my stomach. *Faster*, Xexus, *faster*. With a final surge of astro power, I switch into hyperspeed and vanquish the last morsel into the black hole of inner space.

What's that? Someone is coming into the boys' bathroom. Quick. I've got to stand up on the toilet seat so no one can see my feet under stall number 1. Five, four, three, two, one... *blast off.*

I'm being very quiet now. Standing on a toilet seat isn't easy. Not only am I balancing one foot on either side, but I'm also ducking down so my head doesn't show above the stall. I need to change identities. This is a job for Commando Mucho, top-flight secret spy. Instead of standing on a toilet seat in Lincoln Elementary School, I'm inching my way along a jungle cliff high above the Amazon River. Crocodiles and deadly man-eating piranha fish swim one hundred feet below me in the swirling water.

I creep along the cliff toward the top of a secret banana tree. It's protected by guards with machine guns and bazookas. They don't want anyone to learn the secret of these bananas. But I, Commando Mucho, already know of their superpower. These bananas make anyone who eats them world famous.

My mission is to steal three bananas so our scientists can study them and find out how to grow them. Slowly, without breathing, I look around the edge of the cliff.

"Hey, I smell banana."

Good grief. It's Murray Wallace.

"Is that you in there, Arlo?"

Oh, no, he's detected Commando Mucho. I've got to make my escape. I've got to—*aiyee*. Splash.

Oh, yuk. I've fallen into the toilet. I now have one soaked left foot and shoe. Thank goodness it was flushed.

"It is you, isn't it, Arlo?" Murray asks.

Rats, I'm caught behind enemy lines.

"Hiding in the bathroom eating bananas, huh? How stupid!"

I could really do without this just now.

"There's a school rule against eating food anywhere except in the cafeteria," Murray reminds me. "Only you would think of something as rattlebrained as eating bananas in stall number 1 of the boys' bathroom."

I still haven't taken my foot out of the toilet. He's going to go tell Mrs. Caldwell. I know it, I just know it.

"I'm going to go tell Mrs. Caldwell. We'll see what she thinks of this stupid world-record business!"

I knew it. I just knew it.

"Hold it a minute, Murray," I say in a steady voice. "I want to talk to you."

It's time for Commando Mucho to get out of the toilet and out of stall number 1.

"We have nothing to talk about, Arlo," Murray says as I come out into the open to face the enemy. My left foot and shoe are soggy. My pant leg is wet halfway to the knee. "Tell your story to Mrs. Caldwell. Tell her about eating seventeen bananas in less than two minutes. You can't do it anyway."

I look the enemy in the eye. *No one* tells me I can't.

"You want to bet? Huh, Murray? Do you want to bet on it?" I ask, feeling angry again. "I'll bet you anything I can break the record."

"Anything?" Murray asks.

"Yeah, anything."

"You sure about that, Arlo?"

"Yes, Murray, I'm sure," I say, my eyes drilling into him.

"OK, Arlo." Murray sneers. "You asked for it. Here's a bet for you: if you can't break the world record for eating bananas, then you have to never speak to Laura McNeil again. *Ever.*"

"*What?*"

"That's right, never speak to her again. But

first you have to tell her why: because you're a flop at breaking world records and not worth her time."

"You're weird, Murray," I say.

"I thought you wanted to bet, Arlo," he taunts me. "What's the matter, scared you might lose? Afraid Laura might rather talk to me?"

Someone should do the world a favor and send Murray to Antarctica in a dill pickle jar. He's lucky I'm not a violent person.

I put my hands in my pockets and squint my eyes. "OK, Murray," I say in my toughest voice. "It's a bet. And what if I break the world record? What do you have to do?"

Murray grins. "If, by some strange stroke of luck, you break that stupid record, then I'll do the same thing: not speak to Laura. She'll be robbed of the only real man to be had at Lincoln Elementary School."

"It's a bet, then?" I ask.

Murray nods. "Yeah, it's a bet."

"And you're not going to tell Mrs. Caldwell about me eating a banana in the boys' bathroom?"

"I guess not. Why should I waste my energy getting you in trouble? You seem to have done a pretty good job already," Murray the Nerd says with a laugh, looking at my soaked shoe and pant leg. "After all, what are friends for? Huh, Arlo?"

Friends? *Blaggh*.

CHAPTER 17

"Hemfroph, Mrz. Munoh."
—MIKE SNEAD

Life is hard. I'm sure about that. People like
Murray Wallace help to make it that way. My
bus driver helps, too. I should have known
she'd notice my wet pant leg and shoe. I
should have known she'd bring it to the attention of everyone on the bus by asking loudly
where I'd found such a big puddle to step into.

"That's such a funny sound," she said.
"Squish, thunk, squish, thunk. That's what it
sounds like when you walk with one wet shoe
and one dry shoe."

So now I'm squish-thunking my way across
the wreckage of my bedroom. I've got to clean

this mess up...someday. But right now my mission is clear—I've got to get out of my squish-thunk shoes and pants and get ready for banana practice. Mom is at work, so we are having practice here instead of at Ben's.

Ah...here are my favorite "indestructo" jeans. I keep them tucked back behind my football helmet. Mom doesn't like these jeans. She says I look like a poor orphan with them on. She just doesn't understand. Or maybe she does. But these are the best jeans I own. They're specially equipped with holes in the knees. This allows my bionic kneecaps to see where they're going. These jeans also have a secret pouch inside of the left front pocket. This is perfect for keeping maps and my Case XX pocketknife.

These jeans and I have been through a lot together. They know me. They're good luck. That's why I pulled them out of the garbage when Mom threw them away. That's why they live secretly behind my football helmet in the closet. I only wear them for good luck and when Mom is not around. And today I seem to need all the good luck I can get.

"Hi, Arlo. When does practice start?" Kerry asks. My curly-headed wonder of a sister stands in the doorway with her hands in her pockets.

"Hi, Kerry. Ben said he'd be right over. We'll start when he gets here."

"Good," she says. "I'm ready. Today is the day I spit a melon seed twenty feet!"

"Twenty feet?"

"Yeah," she says, moving over to my bed and absent-mindedly sitting down on my wet school pants. "I made a wonderful discovery at noon recess today. If I throw my head back and then snap my neck forward when I spit, I get twice the distance out of a melon seed. It's all in the snap of the neck."

I yank the wet pants out from under her and put them on the floor where they belong. "Sounds dangerous to me—snapping your neck. Besides, twenty feet isn't even near your goal. You've got to be able to spit over sixty-five feet, right?"

"Yeah, but my new discovery in technique will make all the difference," she says, realizing the seat of her pants is now wet. "You wait and see, Arlo. I can do it."

Seems to me I've heard that before. Sisters don't ever learn.

We're all in the kitchen now—Kerry, Ben, Mike, and me. We moved the table with the plastic orange tablecloth out of the way. Then we began.

I ate two bananas in just over fifteen seconds. Mike gave me a standing ovation. Ben ate two lemons in a little under twenty-five seconds. That's a slower time than he had in the cafeteria a week and a half ago. He said he was just feeling off his best form today. He went home to watch the old reruns of *Leave It to Beaver* and *Bonanza*. Kerry says Ben looks sick to her. "Green around the gills" was how she put it.

Kerry is spitting watermelon seeds across the kitchen. She stands in the hallway door, throws her head way back, arches her body, and then lunges forward in one giant spit. The force of the motion pulls her feet right off the ground and sends the seed zooming across the kitchen and into the living room.

I must admit that I'm impressed with her progress. This neck-snapping method seems to work. She keeps grinning like a dog at a picnic and shouts, "Red alert! Red alert! Melon-seed missile at twelve o'clock." Still, she's only spitting about twenty to twenty-five feet. That's hardly a world record.

Mike has been over by the refrigerator doing jumping jacks and toe touches. He says that warming up is essential to his ice-cream-eating. "If I don't get warmed up first," he reminds me, "I might freeze my stomach with all that ice cream."

Mike has asked for "quiet on the set" so he can concentrate on his speed eating. He is sitting at the kitchen table, staring at a quart of chocolate-chip mint ice cream. I'll time him on Dad's stopwatch.

"OK, Mike," I say, "ready when you are."

He raises his spoon and waves it at me. This is the signal that he's ready.

"Take your mark...get set...go!" I shout and click the watch on.

Wow. Mike is shoveling huge bites of chocolate-chip mint into his mouth. It makes my teeth shiver just to watch him.

"Go, Mike, go! You can do it."

Kerry is Mike's cheering section. All she needs is a couple of pompoms and a megaphone.

"Eat, Mike, eat!...How much time, Arlo?" she asks.

As timekeeper, I must stay cool and observant. "Sixteen seconds and counting."

"Yahoo!" Kerry shouts. "Eat em' up, Mike!"

But as a cool and observant timekeeper, I have failed to notice the time of day or the fact that Mom is now home. Home and standing in the kitchen doorway.

"Hi, Mom," I say, trying not to panic.

"Eek!" says Kerry.

"Hemfroph, Mrz. Munoh," says Mike, greeting my Mom through a mouthful of chocolate-chip mint ice cream.

"Didn't I throw those jeans away, Arlo?" Mom asks, setting two bags of groceries on the counter.

"Well...uh," I stutter, "gee...I'm not sure, Mom." I've been caught in *two* crimes.

"Dinner will be ready in twenty minutes." She's giving me that look again. I'm caught red-handed. "I have a meeting tonight with Mrs. Gorman. I've got to hurry, so supper will be whatever I throw on the stove. Help me with these groceries, please."

Mike is slowly backing toward the door. He still has a huge spoonful of chocolate-chip mint ice cream almost to his mouth. Kerry has snuck into the living room and is frantically picking melon seeds out of the carpet and putting them in her pockets.

"I'm sure I threw those jeans away. You look like a street bum with them on," Mom says with what *might* be a smile on her lips.

Street bum? I thought I looked like a poor orphan child. And why is she not saying anything about what we were doing? I'm *sure* she saw us.

"And don't forget, Arlo..."

Mike has made his escape. I'm not sure if I've made mine.

"It's your turn to set the table..."

Again?

"*After* you throw those jeans away."

CHAPTER 18

"This is the twentieth century, Mr. Macho."
—LAURA MCNEIL

Weekends sure are sneaky. It's almost like being on vacation and driving through a little tiny town out in the middle of nowhere. All you have to do is blow your nose, or spit out your old gum, or pull the crust off your sandwich, and *zip*, you missed it. Missed an entire little town, including a gas station with a bathroom.

Last weekend went by like that for me. One minute it was Friday, then all of a sudden, *zip*, and the weekend was gone.

So now I sit in room 11, Mr. Dayton's fifth-grade classroom. It's Monday, September 19, and I have five days left before the big day. Five days of Positive Brain Approach. Five days of banana practice. Five days until I, Arlo Moore, break the world record for eating bananas and win my bets. My ship is coming in.

Laura turns around in her chair. "Arlo, I need to talk to you."

"Sure. What about?" I ask, gazing at that lovely face, that beautiful hair, those blue eyes that make me dizzy.

"About the bet you and Murray made," Laura says, not smiling.

"The bet?"

"Yes, the bet on who is going to talk to me and who isn't."

There's something about the tone of her voice that makes me nervous. "Oh, that," I say.

"Yes, *that*. It's true, then?" she asks pointedly.

"Well, sort of..."

"Sort of!" Laura looks a bit angry. "Is it or isn't it?"

"Uh...yeah..." I stammer, shifting uneasily in my chair.

"Well, listen to me, Arlo Moore!"

Yep, she's definitely angry.

"I am *not* a prize!"

People are looking over this way.

"Ssh, not so loud, Laura," I whisper, pleading.

"Don't shush me! I am not a prize. No one wins the right to talk to me in a bet. This is the twentieth century, Mr. Macho. Women talk to *who* they want to..."

Oh, boy. I've really blown it.

"...*when* they want to..."

Thank you, again, Murray the Nerd.

"...and *where* they want to!" She glares at me, turns, and picks up her pencil.

There she goes, the girl of my dreams—mad as a bee at a bear.

I'm embarrassed, red as a sunburned baby. I want to shrink to the size of an ant and make a quick getaway.

"Excuse me, Arlo."

It's Mr. Dayton.

"Yes sir," I answer dismally.

"Sorry to interrupt you while you're working so hard on your math. You were working on your math, weren't you?"

"Uh...well..."

"I just received a note from Mrs. Caldwell," Mr. Dayton says. "She would like to see you in her office."

"Mrs. Caldwell? The principal?" I ask like

some kind of idiot. What other Mrs. Caldwell would want to see me in her office?

"Yes, Mrs. Caldwell, the principal," Mr. Dayton replies.

"In her office? Me?"

"Yes, in her office. Now."

This could be bad news on top of bad news.

"Did I do something wrong, Mr. Dayton?"

"I don't know, Arlo. Did you?"

I look at the ceiling and then back at Mr. Dayton. His mustache twitches at me.

"Not that I know of," I say.

"Well, why don't you just go find out what it's all about? I'm sure it's not the end of the world."

Somehow I'm not so sure about that.

CHAPTER 19

"I have information..."
—MRS. CALDWELL

Sitting in the office waiting to see the principal is like having Christmas backward—there's going to be a surprise for me, but I don't think it's going to be a good one.

Mrs. Oatley, the school secretary, is typing at her desk. She's really fast. Every couple of minutes she looks over the top of her glasses at me. I look at something else when she does that. I act interested in the picture of Lincoln Elementary hanging on the wall, or the photocopy machine, or the garbage can in the corner. Then she looks back at her work and begins typing, and I can watch her again.

I think I might learn to type like that. It

looks like fun. I could sit down and bang out letters, and books, and... maybe even a world record. *Yeah,* I'd be the fastest typist alive. I'd type 800 words in one minute. I'd write my life story, and how I became famous. I'd be admired around the globe for my skill. My fingers would dance across the typewriter keys. Laura McNeil would realize what a wonderful person I am. She'd fall in...

"Arlo Moore."

Aiyee, it's Mrs. Caldwell.

"Please come in and have a seat," she says, her voice sounding like a truck in low gear.

I knew it. I can tell. It's Christmas backward. My time has come. Goodbye, cruel world. Slowly I enter her office. Step by step, inch by inch.

"We seem to have a problem, Arlo," she says, sitting down at her desk. I keep standing up. I'm too nervous to sit down.

Mrs. Caldwell still looks like a Japanese sumo wrestler with a dress on. She's been the principal here for eighteen years. I wonder if she's always looked that way.

She stares hard at me with eyes that make me sweat. "I have information that you and a few other students are planning to break world records," she says.

"Well..., yes, Mrs. Caldwell. Is that a problem?" I ask, glancing nervously around her office. The walls are covered with pictures of students and teachers. A rose sits on her desk in a glass vase.

"No," she answers. "Not in and of itself, it's not. Arlo, please sit down. You don't have to stand. Relax."

Why do adults always seem to ask kids to do the impossible? I sit down anyway and try to relax.

"The problem is this, Arlo," she continues. "Benjamin Hamilton is sick."

"Ben? Sick?" I ask. I didn't know that. I thought he had gone to Portland with his mom for something.

"Yes. He's not at school today because of stomach problems," Mrs. Caldwell informs me. "His mother called. It seems that Ben has been eating large quantities of lemons, including the seeds and skin, in an attempt to train for this world-record-breaking event you have scheduled. All of these lemons have made him sick. Too much acid, I think. It's very unhealthy."

"Poor Ben," I say, more to myself than to Mrs. Caldwell.

"Yes, poor Ben," she agrees. "Also, there is a

problem in that Mike Snead is absent from school today."

"Mike, too?" I ask.

"Yes, Mike has a headache. It seems he tried to eat a quart of ice cream in the bathroom this morning before breakfast. His mother reports that he ate so fast that he fainted from lack of oxygen and the cold ice cream. He hit his head on the bathtub and had to have three stitches in his forehead."

"Poor Mike," I mumble.

"Yes, poor Mike," Mrs. Caldwell agrees again. "This, too, I believe, is a result of an attempt to break a world record."

I can feel the winds of doom blowing my way. I'd better try to talk my way out of this. "Mrs. Caldwell, I think—"

"*Also,*" she interrupts like a cannon, "there is a problem in that there is gambling in Lincoln Elementary School."

"Gambling?" I ask. What is she talking about?

"Yes, gambling," she answers. "I have information that there are bets on whether or not you, or Ben, or Mike, or even your sister, Kerry, can succeed at breaking these records."

I look directly at her for the first time.

"Really? People are betting on us?"

"*And* I have information that the betting is spreading."

"Spreading?" I ask with a shiver. Where is she getting her information?

"Yes, spreading! Over thirty students at Lincoln Elementary are betting on the world-record attempts."

"Mrs. Caldwell, I didn't know—"

"Well, now you know, Arlo," she says. I hear anger in her voice. "Now you know that we are not just talking about a world-record attempt. We are talking about students getting sick and hurt. We are talking about gambling at Lincoln Elementary. *And* we are talking about an activity that is interfering with the main reason you are here—to study and learn. Therefore..."

Here it comes. I can feel it.

Mrs. Caldwell leans forward in her chair. Her nose is about eight inches from my nose. I can smell her perfume. "There will be no more betting on attempts at a world record."

"But—" I almost whisper.

"*And* there will be no more practicing for an attempt at a world record."

"But, Mrs. Caldwell—"

"*And* there will be no eating food in an attempt to break a world record at Lincoln Elementary School. Not in the cafeteria, or the classroom, or in the boys' bathroom." She leans even farther forward in her chair. "Is that clear, Arlo?" she asks.

I'm afraid it is. I'd better agree with her—or die at an early age. But *where* is she getting her information?

"Yes, ma'am," I manage to squeak.

"Good," she says, leaning back in her chair and smiling. "I admire your courage at setting a high goal for yourself, Arlo. But it's just as well that this stops now. It is obviously not healthy for young children to eat so much, so fast. And besides, I don't think you could do it anyway. You simply can't."

Can't? Did she say *can't?*

"It's just too much to ask of yourself."

Can't?

"I'm sure we won't have to talk about this again," she continues.

Wrong, Mrs. Caldwell. I *can* break the world record.

"And that there will be no further problems," she says.

I'm going to be in the *Guinness Book of World Records* . . . you can bet on *that*.

CHAPTER 20

"A bet is a bet."
—MURRAY WALLACE

Mom packed a tuna sandwich for my lunch again today. I usually like tuna. But now, sitting in the cafeteria, I'm not hungry. I'm churning inside. I've got a big problem to solve: do I let Mrs. Caldwell tell me what I can't do, or do I do what I believe I can?

My PBA says that I can do it. I can, I can, I can, I can. And I *believe* that.

Mrs. Caldwell tells me I can't. She's the principal. She's in charge. She could get me in big trouble.

But who's supposed to run my life? Me or somebody else? That's the big problem.

"Hi, Arlo. Did you have a good visit with Mrs. Caldwell?"

It's Murray. Murray Wallace, sitting in the cafeteria eating lunch. I didn't even notice him—Murray Wallace who has a smile on his face. Murray Wallace who I'll bet gave Mrs. Caldwell her "information." Murray Wallace the *informer*.

"Thanks a *lot*, Murray," I say, almost spitting the words at him.

"What are you talking about, Arlo?" he asks, acting innocent.

"You know what I'm talking about," I say. "Mrs. Caldwell and her *information*."

Murray smiles at me like a cat smiles at a mouse. "Oh, it was nothing. I'd do it anytime for a good friend."

Friend? *Blaggh!*

"Yeah, well, our bet is off," I say and finally bite into my tuna sandwich.

"Off? What do you mean?" Murray asks.

"It's off," I repeat. "Mrs. Caldwell put the stops on everything—no bets, no world-record attempts."

"A bet is a bet, Arlo, no matter what Mrs. Caldwell says."

"Pig feathers, Murray! It'd be me getting

into trouble, not you."

"Oh, I get it," he says, "you're *afraid* of Mrs. Caldwell. This is your excuse to get out of a bet you can't win. I should have known you'd back out in the end, Arlo. Laura knows the truth—I'm more of a man than you are. It's a plain and simple fact—you *can't* do it."

That does it. It's time for action.

"Can you, Arlo?"

I'm in charge here, Mrs. Caldwell or no Mrs. Caldwell. Rules or no rules. I'm sick of Murray and his mouth. I'll show him once and for all that I *can* do it. Commando Mucho and Xexus of Zoidtron to battle. Five...four...three...two...one...blast off!

"Attention! Attention, everybody!" I yell at the 180 students in the Lincoln Elementary cafeteria. I've climbed up onto a table so I can be seen and heard. The crowd turns.

"You are now about to witness one of the most wondrous events of our time...."

Ooohs and aaahs fill the room.

"I, Arlo Banana Moore, will now give you a show of my world-record-breaking banana-eating skill."

All eyes are riveted on me. This is my finest hour.

"As I eat, not *one*, not *two*, but *three* bananas

in less than twenty-one seconds," I say, pulling the bananas from my lunchbox. "Ready!"

The tension mounts.

"Set!"

The crowd is at the edge of their seats. I'm to be a hero. I can feel it.

"And..."

"Stop right where you are, Arlo Moore!"

Oh, no.

"Get down off that table this instant!"

It's Mrs. Caldwell.

"I'll see *you* in my office, *now!*"

I think I've made a mistake.

"We'll see what your parents have to say about your lack of respect for authority!"

Yes, I've definitely made a big mistake.

CHAPTER 21

"I'll die a true hero."
—ARLO MOORE

During dinner, Mom told Dad about her telephone conversation with Mrs. Caldwell. I sat and stared at my macaroni and cheese. I watched it go from steaming hot to gooey and cold.

Dad didn't say a thing. He just looked at me and then finished eating. Mom "suggested" that I clean up the kitchen while she and Dad talked in the living room.

I've finished cleaning off the table. I've also finished scraping the little bits of macaroni and cheese goo off the plates. I've wiped the orange plastic tablecloth with a wet rag and swept the kitchen floor. And now I'm elbow-deep in suds. I've saved the worst till last. I'm washing the dishes.

I wonder what it would be like to live inside a bubble. This sink is full of suds—thousands, maybe even millions of bubbles. It's like a huge mound of bubble houses.

But who wants to live in a house you can see through? Everyone would know how messy my room is.

Besides, this stuff blows around too easily. I can destroy this bubble mound in one breath. *Whoosh.* The bubble houses go scattering with the force of Hurricane Arlo. *Whoosh.* Thousands of homes are blown over with the force of my hurricane breath. Blasted into the outer reaches of the atmosphere, they fly. Hurricane Arlo keeps them from falling to the kitchen floor. *Whoosh.*

"Arlo."

"Huh? Oh, hi, Dad."

"Quit playing and finish the dishes. Your mother and I want to have a talk with you."

Uh-oh, that sounds serious. I think I'm going to get lecture number thirty-four. That's the one on being honest. Or I might get lecture number twenty-seven. That one covers behaving at school. I'll probably end up getting lectures number thirty-four, number twenty-seven, *and* number forty-three on respecting authority. All this labor in the kitchen, plus three lectures? That seems like too much to me. Mom and Dad have always told us to stand up for what we believe in. That's what I was doing: running my own life, following my own destiny. Is that such a crime?

I'm probably going to have to clean up the kitchen until I'm eighteen years old. All of that dish-washing will give me prune fingers. I won't be able to play soccer or baseball, or peel bananas.

Maybe I could buy an automatic dishwasher. *Yeah.* I'll empty my piggy bank and get one tomorrow. I'll give them eight dollars as a down payment. Then I can use my allowance money to pay on it every week. Mom and Dad will like it so much they'll feel sorry for me.

But it'll be too late. I'll have already been worked to the bone. I, Commando Mucho, prisoner of war, will lie dying in my cell bunk. Doctors will be rushed to my aid. Banana medicine will be flown in from Brazil. My fans will mourn me, but it'll be too late. I'll die a true hero, giving my life for the good of my kitchen. I'll be famous.

And Mom and Dad will feel guilty. They'll be sorry they treated poor Arlo so meanly.

They'll come to the funeral and sit in the front row and cry. "Oh, poor Arlo! Why did we treat him so cruelly? We made him wash the dishes, and scrub and clean. We lectured him. And he was just following his destiny. Oh, poor Arlo!"

"Arlo, are you almost done?" Dad asks from the living room.

Woops, better finish in a hurry.

"Be right there, Dad."

Commando Mucho, prisoner of war, reports as ordered to the firing squad.

CHAPTER 22

"Like a worm on the sidewalk."
—ARLO MOORE

Sometimes I feel like a worm on the sidewalk —confused about how I got there and wondering where I should go.

Here it is, Friday, September 23. I'm sitting alone in my room. Tomorrow is the big day. Tomorrow I go for the official *Guinness Book of World Records* banana-eating challenge— seventeen bananas in less than two minutes. I should be excited. I should be nervous. I should feel confident, or scared, or *something*. But right now I feel like a worm on the sidewalk.

This has been a rough week. Mom and Dad gave me lectures number thirty-four, twenty-seven, and little bits of lecture number forty-three. Dad was very stern. So was Mom. It was serious business. Then they told me that as punishment for my banana-eating and cafeteria crimes, I had to be on kitchen duty for two weeks, plus I had to apologize to Mrs. Cald-well.

I don't mind the kitchen duty so much. I just play with soap bubbles in the sink, chant my PBA, and slowly get the job done.

Apologizing to Mrs. Caldwell was tough, though. I hate to apologize to people, even if they deserve it (which I guess she did).

But it's part three of my punishment that really gets me. It's part three that tastes like sour milk. It's part three that I just can't swallow. They told me I couldn't try to break the banana-eating world record. Dad said I *can't*. Period.

So every day this week, I've become Commando Mucho, top-secret banana-eater and world-record trainee. Mike Snead, Kerry, and I have sworn secret allegiance to our mission. We meet in Ben's garage after school and practice. We *will* attempt our goal. Despite injury, illness, pain, and parents, we will endure.

Mike's stitches came out yesterday. He has a little pink line on his forehead. You can even see the thread holes if you look really closely. He laughs and calls it his "battle scar." But he also told me it aches a little worse than the rest of his head when he eats ice cream really fast.

He can eat a quart of vanilla in less than thirty seconds now. That's good. He's improved. But it's not nearly good enough. He's not going to make it. But he keeps on trying and practicing. I like that about Mike; he's got guts.

Kerry has guts, too. Not only is she still trying hard to spit those melon seeds sixty-five feet, four inches, but she even went out and got a pair of Dad's old boots from the garage. They're huge. She measured exactly twelve inches from the heel of each boot. Then she cut the extra part clean off with Dad's saw. Now, when she spits, she can measure how far the seed went by walking a straight line and putting the heel of the front boot and the toe of the back boot right up against each other. Each step is one foot. She says that's the way *serious* seed-spitters do it.

But Ben is another story altogether, and that's what's got me confused and wondering. Ben quit. He says he can't do it anymore. His stomach just can't take it. He still wants to be my trainer. He still reminds me to do my daily

PBA. And he still lets us use his garage after school. But he quit. They told him he can't, and he believed them. I don't understand. Like a worm on the sidewalk, I'm confused.

CHAPTER 23

"I believe in you."
—MICHELLE ANGIER

Standing before me are my chimpanzees. I see them, thousands of them. They've come to visit the Banana King. Each chimpanzee holds a banana in his hand. As I raise my giant banana above my banana-crowned head, the chimpanzees shriek with delight and do back flips. The time has come. We are ready to begin the Banana Festival.

"Pssst, Arlo..."

Slowly I peel the giant banana. Slowly the thousands of chimpanzees peel their bananas.

"Arlo, wake up."

And I, the Banana King, give the official signal—with a wave of my hand we begin.

"Arlo! Wake up. You're sleepwalking."

"Huh?"

"Wake up," John says. "It's eleven-thirty at night. You should be in bed, not parading around out here in the living room with a banana in your hand and a sheet over your shoulders."

I take a look at myself. Sure enough, I'm standing in the middle of the living room with a banana in my hand and a sheet over my shoulders. John and Michelle are sitting on the couch staring at me.

"Sorry," I apologize, "I thought you were chimpanzees."

Michelle laughs softly.

John looks at me. "No, not the last time I checked. I'm John, your big brother. And this is Michelle, who already thinks I've got a strange family. Do you have to rub it in?"

The TV is on. They've been watching the late-night monster movie—*Godzilla Meets King Kong*.

"Sorry, John. Sorry, Michelle. I didn't mean to—"

"It's OK, Arlo," Michelle says. "I knew I could count on you for a little entertainment."

She looks at John and smiles.

I'm not sure how to take that statement. Entertainment?

"Good *night*, Arlo," John says.

I think he's telling me to vacate the living room.

"Oh, yeah, good night, John. Good night, Michelle," I say with a yawn, then start to turn toward my room.

"Oh, Arlo..."

"What, Michelle?"

She smiles at me. "Good luck tomorrow with your world-record attempt. I'm betting on you."

Wow!

"You are? Really?" I ask.

"Yep. You can do it. I believe in you."

"Gee...thanks, Michelle," I stammer, feeling a little embarrassed.

She believes in me. Michelle believes in me. I *knew* she was smart. She's got "sparkle."

I'm back in bed now. I feel good. I feel *great*. Someone important believes that I can break the world record for eating bananas. And she's almost an adult. This is wonderful.

But what if I *can't* do it? I ate five bananas in forty-three seconds today at Ben's garage. As good as it was for me, it still isn't good enough.

Michelle believes in me, though. Dad doesn't. I'm not sure about Mom. And John sure doesn't. Mrs. Caldwell and Murray the Nerd and a lot of kids at school don't believe I can do it. And worst of all, Laura doesn't. Laura McNeil, the most beautiful girl at Lincoln Elementary School, doesn't believe in me. I'm sure she doesn't. She doesn't even want to talk to me.

But Michelle does. I've got to remember that. Think positive—the Positive Brain Approach. And remember, Arlo Moore, you *can* do it.

CHAPTER 24

"Gazonk!"
—KERRY MOORE

This is probably the most dangerous thing I've ever done. We're all here: Ben, Kerry, Mike, John, me, and even Michelle. We're here even though we're not supposed to be. We're here even though everybody said we can't. And we're here in Ben's garage to witness history being made, to see fame come to Seagrove, Oregon, and hopefully to watch at least one of us claim our rightful place in the *Guinness Book of World Records* (except John, who is here to collect on his bet).

"OK, Mike, you drew the queen of diamonds," Ben says. "That means you go first."

"Aw, c'mon, Ben," Mike pleads, "not me. Not *first*."

Ben looks at me, up at the ceiling, and back at Mike. "Look, we agreed that whoever got the queen would go first. Then whoever got the king would go second, and the ace would go last. You drew the queen. You go first."

Mike lets out a long sigh. "Aw...OK. I guess it's fair," he admits, shifting his weight back and forth from one foot to another. "But why can't Arlo go first? This was his idea to begin with."

"*Mike*, we agreed," Ben reminds him.

"OK, OK...I'll go first. Who's got the ice cream?"

Ben has the ice cream in the big chest freezer they keep in their garage. The freezer is full of frozen beans, peas, corn, orange juice, chicken, beef, and fish. When you open it, an icy fog rises slowly up and around your head. It's like watching the creature of the black lagoon rise out of the murky swamp. Down in the back corner of the freezer are hidden three quarts of Lucerne Old-Fashioned Vanilla Ice Cream. "Pure and natural" it says on the carton. Mike says that if he's going to die from eating too much ice cream, he wants to go naturally.

Ben rises out of the murky swamp with the

three quarts. That's three pounds, six ounces of ice cream. The same amount Tony Dowdeswell ate in 50.04 seconds.

Mike has done his warm-up exercises: jumping jacks and toe touches. He's now sitting in front of a card table. We are gathered around. I've "borrowed" Dad's stopwatch. Ben has it set on zero, point zero, zero.

"OK, Mike, this is it," Ben says solemnly. "You have fifty seconds to eat all that ice cream."

This is just like the Olympics. I can feel the tension in the air before the first big event. Thousands of spectators jam the stadium. Millions watch breathlessly on satellite TV.

Mike has a calm look on his face. He is sitting dead-still. He has his favorite spoon in his right hand, held like a flag in a parade.

Ben starts the countdown. "Take your mark...."

The three quarts of Lucerne Old-Fashioned Vanilla Ice Cream are lined up before him. He is staring at them. I'll bet he's planning his strategy.

"Get set...."

Kerry is in her cheerleader's position. We all take a deep breath. This is *it*.

"Go!" Ben shouts and clicks the stopwatch on.

Mike isn't moving.

"Go, Mike! Go, go, go!" Kerry screams.

Mike still isn't moving.

"Shisk, boom, bah! Go, Mike! Eat, eat, eat!" yells cheerleader Kerry.

Mike *still* isn't moving.

"You're wasting valuable time," yells Ben. "Start eating!"

Mike is now looking at me. He hasn't moved. His spoon is still in his right hand, shining bright, clean, and unused.

"I can't do it, Arlo. You were right," he says in a trembling voice.

Ben has stopped the stopwatch.

"But Mike," I plead, "you trained so hard. You've got to try. At least give it a chance."

"I just can't, Arlo. I tried last night. I only ate two quarts. My head hurt so bad, I thought it was going to split wide open. I just can't do it anymore. I'm sorry."

Silence.

"You've worked hard," Kerry finally says. "That's all that matters. Ice cream is just not the best food for you to eat, that's all."

We all turn and look at Kerry.

"You think so? Really, Kerry?" Mike asks.

"Sure," she says with a wave of her hand. "You should pick a food that doesn't hurt your head—like pancakes or grapes, or...peanuts. Yeah, peanuts!"

Mike's eyes have lit up like a Halloween pumpkin's.

"You know, you're right, Kerry," he exclaims. "Peanuts! I love peanuts! Why didn't I think of that before?"

I'm getting fidgety. I must get this show back on the road. "OK, Kerry, it's your turn to try for your world record. Mike can try peanuts some other time."

"Good idea, Arlo. Let's get ready," Kerry bubbles. "And now, ladies and gentlemen, in the center ring...I will perform at seed-spitting!"

The *Guinness Book of World Records* says that the record for spitting a melon seed under WCWSSA (World Championship Watermelon Seed Spitting Association) rules is sixty-five feet, four inches. This was done by John Wilkinson in Luling, Texas, on June 28, 1980.

Kerry forgot to write the WCWSSA for a set of their rules. She says you just spit, that's all. And if it goes far enough, you win. Period.

"OK, you guys, I'm ready," she says.

My curly-headed sister is standing on the spitting line. She's got on Dad's huge boots with the toe cut off to twelve inches exactly. "My spitting clompers," she calls them. She's so pumped up for this, she's bouncing around like a set of rubber lips.

"Calm down, Kerry," John says. "This is a spitting record you're going for, not a pogo stick contest."

"I know, I know," she assures us. "I'm just getting my energy concentrated. You know, all bundled up into a little power pack. I'm putting it in my throat. Then *pow*, I let it go at exactly the same time I spit. *Zing*, I break the world record."

"Oh, I see," John says, not at all convinced.

And I'm afraid I'm not convinced either. The garage door is open. I can see down the driveway and out onto the street. Mike has his dad's big measuring tape stretched out to the curb. And way out there, about one-third of the way across Holmes Road, I see Ben. He says he's standing on the line that is sixty-five feet, four inches from the line Kerry is standing on. That's how far she has to spit. It's a *long* way.

"Give me the seeds, Arlo," Kerry says.

"Oh, yeah. Here you go—three watermelon

seeds, just like we agreed. You have three chances to beat the record."

"No problem, no problem, Arlo," she assures me, still bouncing in place.

Right...no problem.

"You ready, Ben?" I shout toward the road.

The distant voice returns. "Yep, fire away."

Kerry is concentrating now. She's building up her power pack. Slowly she arches her body. She tilts her head back and puckers her mouth. She looks like an archery bow with big lips. Her eyes squint. She takes a deep breath, and...*ptui,* she snaps forward like a band of steel.

"Twenty-seven feet, nine and one-half inches," Mike yells from halfway down the driveway.

"Good spit, Kerry," I say. "Let it happen, now. Shift into high gear."

"Right, Arlo. No problem, no problem."

Kerry is dancing around like a boxer in the ring. She's all concentrated power pack.

"Ready for number two!" shouts Ben.

"Ready for number two!" relays Mike.

Kerry is on the line again. "I'm ready for number two, you guys. Stand back."

Once again, Kerry arches her body, puckers her lips, and tilts her head back. John, Michelle, and I stand back.

"Do it, Kerry," Michelle whispers.

"Sssh," says John.

Kerry is taking a deep breath. She moans, squints, and... *ptui,* seed number two leaves the launch pad. *Zing,* out the garage door. We hold our breath and wait.

"Thirty-three feet, one inch," Mike reports from the driveway.

"Good, Kerry," I yell. "That was your best yet. You can do it. Let it all go. Don't hold back. Concentrate!"

I'm getting excited. She's really been working at this. What form. What power. Look out, *Guinness Book of World Records!*

"Ready for number three!" shouts Ben.

"Ready for number three!" screams Mike, a little too loud. "C'mon, Kerry, you can do it."

"Give me a second, Arlo. I need to bring forth the power of gazonk."

"The power of what?" I ask.

"Gazonk."

Kerry is dancing around like our dog, Porkchop, when he ate a bee. She's shaking her head and bouncing on her toes.

"What's the power of gazonk?" we all want to know.

"Spit power," she says. "Concentrated spit

power. It's all in the gazonk. I saved it till last. It's my secret helper. Seeds number one and two were just warm-ups. This is it. I can feel it."

I think her hair is getting frizzier.

"OK, Kerry," I say. "Whatever helps. We're ready for number three."

John, Michelle, and I are now backed against Ben's garage wall. Kerry needs lots of room. Bouncing and boxing, she slowly circles up to the line.

"Go, Kerry," Michelle whispers and crosses her fingers. I notice John crosses his fingers, too.

"Good luck, sis," he and I both say at the same time.

Standing with her twelve-inch boots on the line, Kerry arches her back for the third time. If she arched back any farther, I think she'd fall over backward. Maybe those heavy boots hold her to the floor. Her eyes squint, lips pucker, and head tilts. An ear-bonking scream starts low and comes from deep inside my curly-headed, superspitting sister. Watermelon seed number three leaves Ben's garage with a thunderous *gazonk*. *Zing*, and it's gone.

CHAPTER 25

"I can, I can, I can, I can..."
—ARLO MOORE

Watermelon seed number three almost hit Mike Snead. He was thirty-nine feet from the line. It then hit the pavement and bounced once. It skidded to a halt exactly forty-two feet, fourteen and three-quarter inches from where Kerry gazonked it.

We stood in the garage door and looked at Mike, Ben, and watermelon seed number three. And they (except for ol' number three) looked back. Kerry spoke first.

"Not bad, huh, Arlo?"

Not bad was an understatement.

"It may not be a world record," she continued, "but you're looking at the best water-melon-seed-spitter in Seagrove, Oregon, aren't you, John?"

John's mouth was hanging open like mine. "Well... ," he muttered, "I think you're probably right about that."

"That was wonderful!" Michelle exclaimed. And with that, we all started cheering and slapping Kerry on the back and telling her how great she was. She kept saying, "Yes, yes, it's true, isn't it. But really, it was no big deal."

And we all told her that it *was* a big deal, and she was the best in Oregon (maybe), and then...and then I realized that Laura McNeil was also standing in Ben's driveway. Laura McNeil, the most beautiful girl in Lincoln Elementary School. Laura McNeil, who I thought would never speak to me again, whether I broke the world record or not, was standing there in the Saturday-morning sun smiling at me.

"I thought I'd drop by and see how things were going," she said. "For a secret meeting, a lot of people sure know about this, *including* Murray Wallace. He told me he was going to get you guys in big trouble. I thought I should warn you. Murray can be such a...well, a nerd."

Then Laura McNeil smiled at me again, and I melted into a big puddle of Arlo in love.

So now I, Arlo Moore, am sitting in front of the card table in Ben's garage. Seventeen peeled bananas are on a plate in front of me. Seventeen bananas that need to disappear down my throat in less than two minutes. That is, if I'm to break Dr. Ronald Alkana's world record set at the University of California, Irvine, on December 7, 1973.

"Are you ready, Arlo?" Ben asks.

That is the question of the year for me. Am I really ready?

Kerry says, "I did better than I've ever done before, Arlo. You can, too. This is your big chance. This is *it*."

Kerry is right. This is *it*. I've got to do it now. Today is the day. This calls for concentrated effort. This calls for the Positive Brain Approach one more time...for the last time:

I can, I can, I can, I can...

"Remember, Arlo. I'm counting on you. I *know* you can do it."

Michelle...she still believes in me. I've got to do it, I've...

"Me, too, Arlo. You can do it. I know you can."

And Laura, too. *Aiyee*, the pressure mounts. This is a job for Xexus, alien spacebeing from the planet Zoidtron. With PBA, my alien cosmic power, and bionic strength, *maybe* I can do it. Concentrate, Arlo Moore, concentrate.

"Good luck, little brother. Maybe I'll buy you a pizza, huh?"

Even hotshot John is behind me. What magic is this? The powers of Xexus must prevail. For the far reaches of the cosmos, banana lovers around the world, and my now-loyal fans, I must excel.

Ben begins the countdown. "Banana-eater to your mark."

This is really it.

"Get set."

I'm concentrating my brain waves, my alien powers, my training, *all* my banana-eating talents. Five...four...three...two...one...

"Go!" Ben screams.

Hi yo, bananas, away.

"Go, Arlo! Go! Go! Go!" everyone is shouting.

Eating, eating, bananas down into my stomach. Smoothly and quickly, just like I've practiced.

"Yahoo! Eat those bananas!" Kerry screams in my ear.

"Thirty-seven seconds and counting!" Ben yells above the noise of the crowd.

Thirty-seven seconds? I'm behind. I must eat faster.

Kerry is leading the cheering section. "Go, Arlo! Eat, eat, eat!"

My hand is moving faster than my mouth. Xexus of Zoidtron, where are you when I need you?

"One minute!" Ben shouts. "You should be halfway finished. You've *got* to go faster."

Faster? I can't go faster. My stomach is crying out for relief. I'm running out of room for bananas. I've only eaten six.

My fans continue to cheer. "Faster, Arlo. Go! Go! Eat! Eat!"

Come to me, bionic powers. PBA, Xexus of Zoidtron. *Now* is the time. *Down*, bananas, *down*.

It's Ben again. "One minute and seventeen seconds! Keep going, you can do it!"

Aiyee. I'm failing. I feel sick. I feel weak. My stomach is as tight as a drum head. I'm having trouble breathing. I'm chewing so . . . so slow.

"Go, Arlo, go!" Kerry screams. "Hey . . . look, you guys . . . it's Murray. It's Murray Wallace looking through the garage window. He's got a camera. *He's taking pictures!*"

What's all this noise and confusion? Do they realize I can't do it?

"Catch him, you guys," Ben shouts. "He's running for it! He can get us all in big trouble. *Get that camera!*"

Where is everyone going? They've all run out of the garage. I'm here all alone and I feel sick. I don't have any more room in my stomach. I can't eat those last seven bananas.

Tears are running down my cheeks. After all that training, all those bets, all those arguments, PBA, and bananas, I'm finally realizing that Murray Wallace is right—I can't do it.

Can't.

It's that word again. Am I saying that word to myself? No! I hate that word. I've heard that word too many times. I stomp on that word and smash it into tiny banana peels. I grind that word into tiny banana dust. I blow that word into the void of space, flying past Xexus of Zoidtron at the speed of light. *Can't* dies a horrible death at the hands of Arlo Moore.

My time is almost up. I . . . I've got to get rid of these bananas. *Can't* will not destroy me. *Can't* must become *can* . . . Even . . . even if I have to cheat to do it. Yeah, even if I have to cheat.

Down bananas
Down you go,
Where you stop
Only I know.

Into the garbage can
Hidden away,
the world record is mine
today is *my* day.

Can't ... says who?

CHAPTER 26

"You win the bet."
—ARLO MOORE

The Dairy Dip makes an incredible banana split. They start with a perfect ripe banana cut in half and laid in the bottom of an oval bowl. Then comes the ice cream: three scoops, any flavors you want. The toppings are next: hot fudge, little pieces of almonds and walnuts, and mint sprinkles. And last, they put on three big mountains of whipped cream with a cherry on top of each one. It's a masterpiece, a true work of art.

It's Monday afternoon, September 26, and I'm late for my banana split. I should have been at the Dairy Dip fifteen minutes ago. Instead, I'm walking slowly down Twenty-second Street with one foot on the curb and one foot in the gutter. Up, down, up, down, all at a slug's pace.

Kerry, Ben, Laura, Mike, John, and Michelle are all waiting for me. It's supposed to be a celebration party for me—Arlo Moore, world-record-breaker.

Ben was the first one back from chasing after Murray Wallace and his camera. He came flying around the corner and into the garage just as the next-to-last banana disappeared into the big garbage can beside the freezer.

Without blinking an eye, I grabbed number seventeen, the very last banana, and stuffed it in my mouth. And for some strange reason it just slid right down my throat. That banana acted just like it was coated with grease from the hamburger grill at the Seagrove Cafe—zip, slip, and it was gone.

Ben stood wide-eyed, staring at me and then at the stopwatch he still had in his hand. Then he looked back at me and then back at the watch again.

"Turn it off Ben," I said calmly. "I'm finished."

"One minute and fifty seconds!" Ben screamed. "He did it! Arlo really did it! He broke the world record for eating bananas!"

There was a split second right then when I really wanted to tell Ben the truth. I looked up at my best friend standing in front of me, and I really wanted to tell him what I had done with those bananas.

"Look, Ben," I wanted to say. "Those six bananas are in the garbage can. I didn't really break the record. I just tossed them. Out of sight, out of mind, right, Ben? Haw haw. Funny joke, huh, Ben? Haw haw."

And there was an instant when I actually opened my mouth to tell the truth, to admit that I was wrong and I'd cheated to cover it up. That was right before Laura McNeil hugged me, and brother John said, "Well, Arlo, I never thought you could do it. I guess that shows how wrong a big brother can be." I tried to be honest, I really did. The words just wouldn't come out, that's all.

So I just sat there and let Ben keep yelling the news. I just sat there with my mouth hanging open, and without saying a single word, I lied.

Which all brings me to where I now find myself, like it or not, finally standing outside the Dairy Dip. Even if you walk slow, you eventually get where you don't want to be. I feel just as bad today as I did in Ben's garage.

Probably even worse. It seems guilt doesn't go away as quick as indigestion.

I can see them all through the window. Ben, Mike, Kerry, Laura, Michelle, and John. They're sitting around the table by the juke-box. They're waiting for a hero, a world-record-breaker. They're waiting for somebody with *courage*.

Kerry has courage. I never knew it before Saturday, but my frizzy-headed sister is a hero. Not only did she put out a supreme, bionic seed-spitting gazonker (without cheating), but today she took on Murray Wallace. It was won-derful.

Murray walked up to Kerry and me in the hall at school and started bragging about how he was going to get us all in trouble. He held out a roll of film in his hand. Then he told us that he had pictures of everything we did on Saturday.

"You guys have had it," he said. "When I get this film developed, I'm going straight to Mrs. Caldwell and then to your mom and dad with the pictures."

But before I could even open my mouth, be-fore I could even start to beg for mercy, Kerry grabbed the film right out of Murray's hand. "Oh, I love pictures!" she exclaimed. "Let's look at them!" And then, right there in front of Murray, she pulled that exposed film out of the container.

"You ruined it!" Murray yelled. "You exposed it to the light. You destroyed my film, you little twerp!"

Kerry just looked at me and smiled. "See, Arlo. Aren't these beautiful pictures?" she said. I had to agree with her. They were indeed beautiful.

"You'll pay for this, you little twerp!" Murray kept yelling. "If you weren't a little fourth-grade nerd, I'd...I'd...I'd pound you into the pavement!"

That's when Murray grabbed the ruined film out of Kerry's hand and stomped down the hall yelling over his shoulder. "You'll pay for this, *both* of you! You haven't heard the last of Murray Wallace!"

Mrs. Caldwell sure looked strange when Murray slammed into her. She had walked out of her office, probably to see what all the yelling was about, just as Murray got there, still yelling over his shoulder. Her eyes popped wide open in surprise. Her mouth flew open like she was going to scream, but no noise came out. She and Murray both sailed through the air in slow motion, just like in the movies.

They hit the floor at the same time and slid into the office door before they stopped.

Mrs. Caldwell jumped up faster than I've ever seen her move. She grabbed Murray by his hair and yanked him into her office so fast I felt the breeze from thirty feet away.

I think we may have finally heard the last of Murray Wallace.

"Hey, Arlo. What are you doing standing out there? Come on in."

Aiyee. Ben has spotted me. It's too late. I've got to go in. I'm now walking inside the Dairy Dip like a traitor to the gallows. I'm doomed.

"Hey, you guys. Look who's here," Ben says with a big grin. "It's Arlo Moore, world-record-breaker."

I can't stand this.

"Yay, Arlo!" everyone cheers.

"Great, Arlo! Way to go," Kerry shouts (of course).

"Have a seat, champ," Mike says, offering me a chair.

"You did it, Arlo! I knew we could count on you," Michelle says, giving me a hug. Laura just smiles her big, blue-eyed, warm, fuzzy smile.

This is too much. I need to shrivel to the size

of a mosquito. I need to be swatted like a buzzing little pest. That's what I deserve.

"And guess what, Arlo?" Ben asks.

Please, nothing more. Let me just dribble down a drain and flow into the ocean.

"What, Ben?" I ask. "I don't feel like guessing."

"The letter came today!" he exclaims.

"The letter? What letter?" I ask.

"You know. The letter from Norris McWhirter, editor and compiler of the *Guinness Book of World Records*. It came in the mail today. It's probably got all the information in it on how to prove that you did what you did, right, Arlo?"

I fiddle with my jacket zipper. Guilt is bouncing through my body, cringing my nose, elbow, and toes.

"I thought you should open it since you're the champion," Ben continues. "Here, you do the honors," he says, handing me the letter.

He means cheater. I'm a cheater, not a champion. Nobody needs to prove that to the *Guinness Book of World Records*.

"Go on, Arlo, open it," Laura says, looking at me with her bright blue eyes and wonderful smile.

I can't go on anymore. I can't stand this. I look at them and try to talk. "Hey, you guys . . . Ben . . . Laura . . . Kerry . . . Mike . . . John . . . Michelle. . ."

This is terrible. I feel like a kick starter on a mule, a complete waste of everybody's time.

"What is it, Arlo?" Kerry asks. "Why aren't you opening the letter? Are you feeling OK?"

If she only knew—but that's *it*. She *should* know . . . they *all* should know . . . and I've got to tell them . . . now.

I finally speak. "I've got to tell you something . . . about Saturday . . . and the world record . . ."

"What is it, Arlo?" Michelle wants to know. "We're listening."

Here goes. Goodbye, friends. Goodbye, family. *Goodbye, cruel world.*

"I cheated," I say softly, my voice hoarse.

Silence.

"You what?" Ben asks.

"I . . . I cheated on Saturday. I didn't really eat seventeen bananas in less than two minutes."

Silence. Silence. And more silence. I'm no longer human. They'll never speak to me again. I'm a cheater. I deserve it.

I go on. "And I want to apologize to all of you. I cheated and I lied. And I don't deserve a party."

Silence.

I think I'll go shrivel up and crawl into a crack in the sidewalk.

I get up to leave. "Goodbye. See you guys later...maybe."

And so I leave my former happy life. Dragging heavy feet toward the door, I face guilt and shame forever.

"See, I told you he'd come through in the end," I hear Michelle say.

What's this? Who is she talking about?

"Yep, you were right, Michelle, you win the bet," John says.

What bet? What in the name of a monkey's elbow is he talking about?

"I was beginning to wonder myself," says Kerry. "I thought he'd never level with us."

They're talking about *me*. They're talking about Arlo Moore, cheater and liar supreme.

"Not me. I was sure he would," says Laura. "He just needed a little time, that's all."

"I told you so," says Ben. "I've known Arlo for a long time. We go way back. When I found those bananas in the garbage can, I knew he would eventually tell the truth. He just needed some time, that's all. He's a great banana-eater but a lousy liar. Right, Arlo?"

The garbage can. So they know. They all know I threw the bananas away, that I cheated.

But they're smiling. They're looking at me and they're *smiling*.

"Right, Arlo?" Ben asks again, his grin getting even wider.

Nobody forgives what I did...do they? Sausageheads like me don't get smiles. We get pelted with open-faced peanut butter sandwiches and squirted with slug juice...right?

"Come back here and sit down, Arlo," says Mike Snead. "We're going to eat some ice cream, and we're going to eat it S-L-O-W."

EPILOGUE

"When I think about it, I guess she's right."
—ARLO MOORE

I still eat bananas sometimes. I like to sit up in the big pine tree on a warm day and slowly peel that luscious fruit, and eat it inch by inch, bit by bit... carefully... in slow motion. And I imagine that I'm a chimpanzee, with nothing to do but be lazy and pretend I'm Kerry's ten-year-old brother in disguise.

Every now and then, when the sun is shining and a warm breeze is blowing off the ocean and singing through the needles of the big pine, I think about breaking a world record.

I can close my eyes and see myself doing it. I can hear the fans yelling my famous name. I can smell the aroma of roses and I can taste victory. And I really think I could do it.

But I don't talk about any of that to anybody. That's just between me, the big tree, and my new edition of the *Guinness Book of World Records*.

And if I do try again, it'll be for the fun of it and because it makes me feel good to try. That's all. No bets. No cramming food down my throat. No indigestion. No weird me driving my fifth-grade brain bananas. And for sure no lies.

I've paid off all of my bets. Kerry said she wanted watermelons instead of banana splits. She now has a set of the official World Championship Watermelon Seed Spitting Association rules. Almost any sunny afternoon you can find her spitting and clomping around the backyard in her twelve-inch spitting boots. Mike Snead eats peanuts and watches. Kerry is practicing for next year's national spitting contest in Luling, Texas. Dad says no. Mom smiles and calmly says, "We'll see." Kerry says, "Gazonk! Gazonk!"

Laura McNeil and I sit next to each other in Mr. Dayton's fifth-grade class, room 11. She told Murray Wallace that she would talk to whomever she wants to, no matter who won our bet, and that she definitely didn't want to talk to him. Ben snickers and says I'm in love. That's when I usually punch him in the arm.

John got his pizza. He and Michelle and I went out to Papa Dietro's for an extra large supreme pizza, which I paid for. My piggy bank is now empty. But John had to pay for the Cokes. That's what he gets for betting Michelle that I wouldn't tell the truth about cheating instead of eating. Michelle says she believed in me. She says she knew I could do it. And when I think about it, I guess she's right.

Who knows . . . I might even be famous someday.